Certain Revenge

a novel by
Dragan Tupaic

Dragan Tupaic
St. Kanona A. R. 1,
Korcula 20260, Croatia

+385.98.1655.914
Email: dtupaic@gmail.com

ISBN 978-953-57951-1-7
eISBN 978-953-57951-0-0

Contents

Chapter 1: The Dock 1
Chapter 2: Coming to America 3
Chapter 3: Young Genius 7
Chapter 4: College Days 11
Chapter 5: Romancing Lady Luck 19
Chapter 6: Lady Luck Flies Away 25
Chapter 7: Lottery Heist 33
Chapter 8: The Genius and Pete 45
Chapter 9: The Setup 53
Chapter 10: Bank Heist 67
Chapter 11: Genius Revenge 79
Chapter 12: Payoff 87
Chapter 13: The Dock, Revisited 89

Chapter 1

The Dock

The warm Sicilian sun cast lengthening shadows across the dock as the afternoon wore on. Tourists, just off the ferry boat from the big cruise ship anchored offshore, scattered in search of places to dine and shop the evening away. Now, the locals had reclaimed their dock, hoping to catch a breath of cool evening breeze, and grateful that the tourist rush was nearly over.

Helen Palmer, the former Lady Attenborough, wrapped in tweedy elegance from London's best boutiques, strolled one last circuit of the dock, trailed by her daughter Charlene. Helen's patrician jaw was set in grim resolution; she vowed to make the best of a holiday that was fast turning to shit. If only her husband, the film producer Richard Palmer, would get his rich American arse out of the cruise ship's casino! Instead, Lady Helen found herself alone, handling the job of keeping their budding daughter safe and virginal—a daunting task with all these Italian wolves around.

As the mother and daughter neared the end of the dock, they passed a group of local boys lounging on the weathered planks, idly chatting and tossing pebbles into the water. The boys followed Charlene with their eyes, but they'd barely wet their lips for the obligatory wolf-whistle when Helen's fierce glare silenced them. Turning back to the water with a giggle, they missed Charlene's exaggerated eye roll.

The two women paused at the end of the dock, looking out to the horizon. Charlene sighed, bored and uncomfortable in the fashionable clothes she'd been so pleased with earlier in the day. She envied the carefree local youths, boys and girls, enjoying the fine summer's day in their casual T-shirts and shorts. The breeze picked up and ruffled the women's hair. Charlene dug in her handbag for a comb, then gasped as her silver wallet—from the latest Prada collection, no less—slipped out of her bag. The wallet bounced off the dock and disappeared into the water.

Before either of the women could cry out, the tallest boy in the group near them jumped up and dove into the sea. He swam beneath the waves and surfaced seconds later, holding Charlene's wallet in one hand. Then he paddled back and scrambled onto the dock in one fluid motion.

"Per voi, signorina," said the boy.

Charlene smiled, her arms opening as if to hug him. But Helen broke in with a muttered *"Grazie,"* and yanked her daughter away from the helpful but uncouth local. As her mother dragged her down the dock to the ferry that would return them to another dull evening on the cruise ship, Charlene looked back, hoping to catch the eye of the handsome lad who'd saved her wallet. But the tall Italian youth wasn't looking at her. He was staring at the cruise ship, lost in wonder and dreams.

After snapping out of his daydream about the cruise ship, Tony realized the blond girl and her mother have already boarded the ferry that would take them to the cruise ship. As he lowered his head in disappointment, something caught his attention: by the edge of the dock was the beautiful girl's silver wallet. She must have dropped it as her mother dragged her to the ferry.

He picked it up and frantically waved his hand, but the girl was no longer in sight.

Ciao . . .

Chapter 2
Coming to America

The silence that filled the Donatelli kitchen that evening was broken only by the sobbing of Maria, Tony's mother. His father Paulo, looking even more glum than usual, quietly sipped a glass of grappa as he watched his wife reach for another embroidered handkerchief. Their last child was leaving home tonight for New York with his uncle, Marco Milione. No matter how long they'd known this day was coming, they could never be prepared for it. Paulo clumsily patted Maria's hand in an effort to comfort her, which only made her cry harder.

Marco entered, dressed like he was headed to an American disco. Marco and Tony would be sailing to New York aboard the *Bella Lucia*, the official launch of the Milione Casino—his main enterprise, one out of many.

Maria stopped her crying just enough for an expression of disgust to cross her face, but Marco took no notice as he embraced his brother and thumped him on the back.

"Fratellino," murmured Paulo, "take good care of *mio figlio."*

"Don't worry, Paulo; don't cry, Maria." Marco bent and kissed his sister-in-law's salty cheek. "You know I am keeping my promise to *Padre Nostro.* Tony will do well in America; I'll see to it. And when he does, I'll make sure he sends back money for your old age, and nice things you can't get here, including pretty dresses for his mamma."

Maria smiled faintly. A little flattery works for all women, even the country drudge his brother had married. Marco glanced at the expensive Rolex strapped to his wrist.

"Tony, where are you? It's time to leave."

Tony had finished packing and was out behind the house, leaning over the fence to steal grapes from the neighboring lodge. The sweet Sicilian grape was his favorite, and he greedily ate the ripe fruit for what he thought would be the last time. Hearing the calls coming from the kitchen, he sighed and licked his fingers. He picked up his luggage and walked into the kitchen carrying the suitcase that held all of his possessions. He put it down as he went to kiss his parents for the last time. "Good-bye, Mamma, Papa. Don't be sad. I'll write you. I promise. You'll see!"

The family walked out into the yard, where Marco's cream-colored Mercedes was waiting. After stowing Tony's luggage, uncle and nephew climbed in. Marco started the engine and smiled as the bouncy sound of Italo Disco came through the speakers. As much as he loved his brother, he'd had enough of the old-country ways for this visit. They waved good-bye as Marco put the car in gear and rolled out of the driveway.

***

The Mercedes pulled into a parking space by the dock where the *Bella Lucia* was anchored. As they got out and removed their luggage, Tony briefly wondered if the blond tourist girl from yesterday and her stuck-up mother would be there. He felt for the silver wallet safely tucked in his messenger bag. *I need to return this to her.* But the cruise ship had sailed on, and Tony forgot about the girl as he took in the view of the luxurious yacht he was about to board.

An assistant to the parish priest was there waiting. Marco tossed the Mercedes' keys to the assistant, who was tasked to drive the car back to the parish church. It would be Marco's gift to the parish: his first car that he'd bought in America with the profits from the Milione Casino. With money enough that he wanted for nothing, Marco felt compelled to give something back to this dusty corner of Sicily that would forever be the land of his ancestors. Besides, he felt that giving up his prized Mercedes would keep his run of good luck alive. Fortune didn't favor anyone of her children for very long.

He led his nephew up the gangplank and into the yacht's teak-lined interior. The ship's salon boasted a bar of solid mahogany, and the tables were constructed out of white pine to Marco's "Milione" specifications. "Breathe that," he said as he inhaled deeply. "There's nothing like that white pine smell."

He turned to watch the porters bringing aboard the last of their luggage. Then two more porters came aboard, pushing dollies stacked with sturdy wooden crates. Marco stopped one of the porters and directed him to open the top crate. Tony, watching, was dazzled by the cargo: rows of precision Italian rifles that filled the crate. Marco nodded in satisfaction and closed the crate.

"It's a shame these beautiful guns have to ride in the freezer," he said with a wink to Tony, who gave him a quizzical look. "Didn't you read the label on the crates? 'Mediterranean Seafood Company.' The Feds think we're shipping fish and crabs—let them! The taxes are a lot cheaper that way."

They stepped out onto the deck, and Marco pulled Tony over to the rail, looking back at the land they were leaving. "Look well, Tony, at our island of Sicily. We were born here. This is our land. This is the place where our mothers and fathers were born before us. We belong here. And we always will."

The yacht cast off and began moving away from the dock and out to sea. The ship's mechanic joined them. *"Benvenuto,* Marco, is this your nephew?"

"Si. Carlo, this is my nephew Tony."

The mechanic offered to show the boy around the yacht, and Marco followed. They went down to the engine deck, and Tony looked fascinated at two huge metal balls that were slowly moving—the ship's gyroscope.

"These balls stabilize the ship, so it won't sway," Carlo pointed out. "There are a lot of Italian inventions and industry in ships, you know? Do you want to come and work on a ship?"

At that moment, Tony would have liked nothing better, but his uncle intervened. "Nah, Tony has a job to do in America."

The *Bella Lucia* docked in the early-morning light at the Milione Company's Atlantic port. As their journey neared its end, Marco's mood had grown more reflective. He began keeping a journal, and, on that last morning at sea, he made aimless jottings while sipping his coffee. His nephew Tony could hardly contain his excitement and nearly had to be restrained from jumping off the ship and onto the dock. Watching the boy and his enthusiasm prompted Marco to pick up his pen and write:

> *Tears are no longer sufficient to describe the expression of those people who stepped off the ship onto the big island and continent of America. They felt as though their hearts had stopped for a minute, but suddenly the amazement of that new wide world struck them. They instantly knew that this was the Promised Land.*

Chapter 3
Young Genius

A fternoon light glinted off the modern Danish furniture in the Nielsens' living room. Deep in his work on the Amiga computer—kick-ass for gaming and years ahead of its time—young Gustav didn't hear his mother enter.

"Figlio, cosa stai facendo?"

Gustav sighed. His mother was determined to preserve her native Italian come hell or high water. "I'm working on the computer, Ma," he replied out loud. *As you can obviously see,* his brain answered for him.

Gustav was growing up in isolation—his computer as his only companion, and hacking as the only form of enjoyment. He had no friends, and neither did he desire any.

"Må din krop roterer med prutter!" shouted Gustav's father, Niels. The angry voices of his father and the next-door neighbor drifted in through the open window. The boy chuckled, trying to imagine the neighbor's fat body rotating with farts. The Danish language was good for cursing.

That evening, Niels switched channels on the TV, pausing curiously at an ad for the video game *Hugo.* Kids loved the game, because they got to help an animated troll named Hugo rescue his wife, Hugolina, and their kids from the various evils of an enchanted forest. The game was played by pressing the dial keys on a telephone. Niels shook his head. *Imagine those phone bills,* he thought. *What a waste of money!*

Gustav watched, too. He was intrigued by the advanced technology of the animation. The voice actor for the troll Hugo wore sensors on his face. As he voiced the troll's dialogue, the sensors relayed his movements to the animated Hugo, who then made facial movements that seemed extremely realistic—especially for a cartoon fantasy character.

"Du bliver aldrig fri fra Hugo," cackled the voice of the wicked witch Afskylia. *You will never forget the* Hugo *game.*

"That looks like fun, Dad," said Gustav. "I want to play!"

"We can't afford it, Gene," replied his father.

"Why do call you me that, Dad?"

"Because you're a genius," replied Niels, in English. He grinned. "And it will be good for you to have an American name when you go to college in America. Now, you'd better get studying, so you can win that scholarship!"

Gustav/Gene waited in his room until he heard his parents snoring down the hallway. Pulling a telephone wire from the wall, he twisted two wires together. Sparks flew. He dialed the number for *Hugo.* The game show came to life on his small TV set. He flipped a switch to change from pulse to tone dial and pressed the "4" key on the phone's dial pad. The mine car in the video game turned to the left. He pressed the key once again, grinning as the car on the screen flew off the bridge. *Pretty cool,* he thought. *I like that MT8888 microchip.* His agile mind blossomed with ideas for more uses of the MT8888's capabilities as a dual-tone multi-frequency transceiver.

He opened a small notebook that he used to write down his best gaming moments. After making notes about this triumph, he flipped back to the cover page that he'd labeled with his name. Taking up his pen, he crossed out "Gustav" and wrote "Gene." He smiled. *I really am a genius,* thought Gene.

***

Gene slouched in his chair as the school's computer science teacher droned on about Univac, punch cards, mainframes—yadda yadda. He'd known this stuff for ages, why should he be forced to listen to it again? His Amiga computer at home would stump that fool of a teacher if she ever tried to use it!

Staring out the window, Gene watched the cars going by on the road past the school. His thoughts wandered two seasons back, to the best adventure he'd had with his pal Arne. Arne had been showing off his model car styled after a Formula 1 racer, and Gene persuaded him to lend him the miniature for a little fun.

Pulling a detonator cap out of his pocket, Gene said, "Let's replace the engine with this."

Arne watched as Gene carefully disconnected the wires, inserted the detonator capsule, and began the reconnection. "Which one, blue or red?" asked Arne.

"There is no blue or red," smiled Gene. "You've been watching too many stupid movies. Blue or white? Makes no difference. When you cut the electrical circuit, the circuit opens; the current doesn't flow anymore." He finished with the wires, replaced the batteries, and set the car down on the curb. "Let's see if the headmaster's car is coming this way like usual."

Sure enough, the headmaster's big-finned behemoth came barreling down the roadway from the school. "Now, duck," Gene instructed Arne as he activated the remote control and fiddled with the joystick. The model car moved along the curb and slid down into the gutter, then exploded with a flicker and a *BOOM!* exactly opposite the front wheels of the headmaster's car.

The car stopped, and the headmaster slowly got out, regaining his dignity after the noise had startled him. He looked at the tires and found nothing, except some plastic bits and pieces near the gutter. Shaking his head, he slowly got behind the wheel and continued on his way. Meanwhile, Gene and Arne, having ducked behind a conveniently large tree next to the road, were frantically trying to stifle their laughter.

The look on the headmaster's face had been priceless, Gene thought as he focused on his school notebook opened on the desk in front of him. He picked up his pencil and began to sketch the toy car as it had looked with the wires hanging out of it. Silence took over the classroom as the teacher's voice stopped.

Gene felt a presence hovering over him. He slowly looked up into his teacher's angry face, her eyes boring in his.

"Well, that's a very nice drawing, Mr. Nielsen. Can you possibly tell us what it has to do with the computer history topics we've been discussing?"

Gene was caught. Passive resistance was his best option. "No, ma'am. It doesn't have anything to do with the class discussion."

Taken aback by Gene's admission of guilt, the teacher let her fight drain away. "Well ... I do hope you will have your term paper completed by tomorrow. It's been assigned for three weeks, you know."

Gene had not started on it. "Yes, ma'am, I will."

"And you will have it all typed in the proper format and filed in the class computer folders?"

"Of course I will," answered Gene. "I'm a computer genius."

***

Gene was late getting home, and his parents had gone out to dinner. He'd been kept after school to answer more interminable questions from the computer science teacher. He let himself into the darkened house and dropped his backpack by the door, then headed to the kitchen to make a grab-and-eat snack. Fortunately, his mom overcame her Neapolitan sensibilities enough to buy American food for her son to gobble when starving. Taking his peanut-butter sandwich and glass of milk to the table, he wolfed down half his meal before noticing the thick envelope with his name on it on the table in front of him. He wiped his hands and opened it. It was from his top-choice university in America:

Dear Mr. Nielsen, we are pleased to inform you that your application for admission has been accepted ...

Chapter 4
College Days

*F*ascino! declared the blinking neon sign above the small table where Tony Donatelli and his *compagni* were sipping glasses of house red. Tony tapped out a text message on an older-model tablet.

"Hey, Tony," ventured Silvano, one of his friends. "When you gonna trade that in for a newer model? It's only been what—decades—since you lifted it."

"Hell, it's not even three years old," answered Tony, getting in the mood. "The newer ones, they're for shit." Tony winked, and the boys chortled on demand. They would always laugh at Tony's favorite stories, no matter how lame. And besides, his uncle was the boss.

They returned to eyeing the female contingent of the college crowd gathered at the popular hangout. Two girls walked by their table, one blonde and one brunette. They gave haughty glances to the source of the catcalls and *Bella, bella!* from the Italians' table. "Come here and listen to some Italo Disco with us," offered Tony, but the girls just blew them a kiss and walked out the door.

Tony's mood darkened. He finished his wine and tapped the glass on the table. "Well, boys, I'm done for tonight," he said, pushing his chair back. "And anyway I have an exam tomorrow."

***

Clutching their take-away coffee orders, the bleary-eyed students filed into the amphitheater-style classroom. *Midterm Exam* was scrawled on the front chalkboard in oversized letters. Tony looked around nervously from his seat near the front, hoping one of the smart kids would sit next to him. Of course, he wouldn't cheat, he told himself, but maybe some of their smarts would rub off by proximity.

The bell sounded, and the professor and his teaching assistants began handing out the exam booklets. A few latecomers hurried to the empty seats. Among them, Tony noticed, were the two girls from last night at Fascino. And they seemed to be heading his way. In fact, the blonde was gesturing to her friend that she wanted the seat next to Tony, and there she settled.

"I have no idea how I'm going to make it through this exam," she whispered with a smile to Tony.

Well, baby, if you plan to copy off my paper, you're in trouble, Tony thought. Still, he couldn't deny she was attractive, even exotic-looking with her long straight hair that flowed over her shoulders, held back by a tiny silver chain she wore as a headband. Then he forgot about her as he opened his exam packet and read the questions.

***

Gene Nielsen sat near the back of the exam room. No matter how hard he'd argued with his advisor, there was no way out of the requirements of his scholarship. He had to take Computer Sci 101, even though he'd been dealing with this stuff since he was ten. While he waited impatiently for the exams to be handed back to his row, he watched the other students file in and take their places. That blond girl he'd had his eye on came in with her friend. For a moment, Gene thought she was heading towards him, but instead she sat next to that tall, dark-haired guy. Bummer. Gene read his exam questions and started checking off the answers.

***

Tony sweated his way through the exam, doing his best to avoid being distracted by the blonde who'd been trying to catch his eye throughout. Jesus, didn't she have to pass the exam, too? Now, she was flipping the ends of her hair and giving him sideways glances. With forty-five minutes left in the exam period, Tony had passed the halfway point but still had three pages of questions to answer. He was staring at the clock over the stage at the front of the room when the first student walked up and handed in a finished exam.

It was that geeky kid with the weird accent named Gene something-or-other. Tony made a mental note as he watched Gene saunter out of the room. *I'd better chat up that guy the next time I see him,* he thought. *If the rest of the exams are like this, I'm going to need some help to get through this course.*

Finally, the exam was over. Tony filled in his last answer a bare minute before the ending bell. The blond chick had left just minutes ago, whispering *"Fascino"* in his ear as she got up to hand in her papers. *Not a bad idea,* Tony thought as he handed his answer sheet over to the student proctor. With the exam over, Tony headed to Fascino to unwind. It was too early for his gang to show up, but he was thinking maybe somebody else—someone much more attractive—would join him.

Sure enough, by the time he'd settled down in the game room with his glass of house red, the blonde who'd sat next to him entered and surveyed the room. Seeing Tony, she let loose with a million-dollar smile and walked over to him.

"Tony? Hi, I'm Charlene."

"Nice to meet you, beautiful Charlene." How the hell did she know his name?

"Thanks. By the way, I got your name from the top of your test paper. And that's the only thing I took from it, I swear!" She laughed, standing at near attention and giving him a humorous Girl Scout salute.

In a flash of a brief memory, he remembered that she was the beautiful girl he had retrieved the wallet for. Amazing! What a small world! "Good. I'd hate to think of you flunking out!" They wandered over to the back of the room where the dart boards were set up. Tony threw some darts, hitting the bull's-eye on the third try. He handed a set of darts to Charlene. "Here, try it. If you hit the bull's-eye, that means we'll be together forever." Charlene smiled and threw the dart.

Bull's-eye.

***

Gene adjusted the badge he wore, identifying him as "Staff - Computer Center." He'd Photoshopped it the night before and had it laminated at a copy center near the campus. *Not bad*, he thought. At least it got him past security, at the entrance to the admin building, and into the university's computer center.

It was late in the day, and several weeks after the midterm exam. As expected, he'd aced the test with 100 percent correct answers. Boring. Then, at the next class meeting, the Italian guy, the one who'd been seen around talking to the blond chick, started getting chummy. What the heck, at least the dude was springing for expensive coffee as he picked Gene's brain. It was a hell of a lot better than the cheap swill Gene could afford on his scholarship budget, so he was happy to drop a few pointers Tony's way. He'd never catch up to Gene in the grade rankings, anyway.

The computer center seemed deserted. Gene scanned his badge, and the door opened for him—first obstacle overcome. He thought back to how he'd gotten involved in this escapade. After chatting him up for a week or so, Tony started dropping hints that he could use Gene for more than just a study hall partner—and he could pay more than just a free coffee now and then. Gene took the bait, and here he was, breaking into the university's secure computers—for the few hundred bucks he needed to pay next month's rent.

Why am I doing this? Gene asked himself as he sat down in front of an active computer monitor. He slipped on a pair of those plastic gloves that a janitor or a dentist would use, and tapped the SHIFT key a couple of times. The monitor lit up, and Gene went through the login hack he'd developed the day before. *I'm doing it for the challenge,* he reminded himself. The hell with the money, Gene just wanted to see some action. If he didn't get some mental exercise soon, his brain would start growing cobwebs.

A few more keystrokes on that Apple II Computer with BASIC software, and it was done. The names Tony Donatelli and Charlene Palmer had shifted position towards the front of the class list. They'd both gotten an *A-* on the midterm. Imagine that.

Gene let the monitor go dark and checked to make sure he hadn't left anything out of place at the work station. His badge scan worked again to let him out of the computer center, and he retraced his steps out of the admin building, stopping first at the men's restroom to leave the gloves buried in a waste can full of used paper towels.

Repeated hacks by Gene guaranteed Tony and Charlene of passing their senior year with flying colors.

***

In the last week of his senior year, Tony sat in a coffee shop near the campus, sipping a halfway decent cappuccino. His uncle Marco had taught him well. He knew the finer points of coffee connoisseurship. Tony watched Gene carrying a venti-caramel-something to their table. What a leech. Gene always ordered those expensive sugary drinks when it was on Tony's nickel. Too bad he felt so dependent on Gene for his grades.

"Sit down, Gene, and enjoy your breakfast," Tony said with a thin smile. "In a few days, we'll be college graduates. What do you think of that?"

"Um, okay I guess," Gene shrugged. He sipped his coffee and bit into the Danish roll he'd also purchased courtesy of Tony.

"You got plans for after we graduate?"

"Not really. Thought I'd take some time off, maybe do an internship." *If I can get one,* Gene thought. He knew his job search had been less than diligent. His own grades had fallen since he'd started helping Tony—and Charlene as well—with their grade "issues." Funny thing, hacking into the university computer wasn't exactly something you could highlight on a resume. "What about you?"

"Oh, I don't worry," Tony answered. "Uncle Marco has a place for me, I'm sure."

Must be nice, Gene thought.

"We can probably find something for you, too," Tony continued. "Something that would make good use of your considerable talents."

"Umm, okay."

"Well, I gotta go. Call me in a week or so; let's see what we can do."

"Yeah, sure. Ciao." *Whatever.* He was counting the days until he'd be done with the grade-fixing for Tony and Charlene. If he'd just had to raise Tony's grade, it wouldn't have bothered him. But the directive to boost Charlene's grade as well gnawed at his gut. He hated any reminder that the two of them were an item. Gene knew he wasn't in Charlene's league—she barely knew he existed. But he could dream— until reality came crashing down on him every time he scrolled for her name on the computer screen.

At least it would soon be over. Gene took another bite of the Danish roll and opened his computer magazine to the classified section. *Hmm, not many listings this week.*

***

Among the luxury hotels lining the Jersey shore, only one remained dark. There was just enough light from the security and parking lights for Tony and Gene, both wearing dark clothing with caps pulled low on their foreheads, to pick their way through the shrubbery to the building's side entrance. Some weeks ago, Gene had reluctantly made that phone call to Tony. It was easier than sending out yet another batch of resumes that would end up in some corporate recruiter's round file. And besides, night owl that he was, Tony's flexible requirements fit better with Gene's laid-back lifestyle.

"You know why this resort was built?" whispered Tony, leading the way.

"No idea."

"Money laundering. No tourists, but the books show thousands of reservations."

"I guess you would know. Aren't the owners part of your family?"

Tony snorted. "Third cousins, twice removed. Now a rival gang, if you can call them that."

"So is that good or bad for us?"

"The good news is, they won't report their losses to the cops. The bad news: if they catch us . . ." No words were needed, but Tony drew his finger across his throat for good measure.

He handed Gene a pair of dark gloves, and started to pull a similar pair onto his own hands. "Do I need gloves?" he mused. "They make me look like a dock worker."

He dropped the gloves on the floor and said to Gene, "No talking from here on. I know how to find the safe. Are you sure you can decode the lock mechanism?"

"Piece of cake."

And it was: Gene placed a super-magnet on the door frame, opposite the alarm system's magnetic switch, to trick the switch into "thinking" the door remained undisturbed—even as they opened it and entered. Then he altered the wiring connections to keep the mercury-filled tilt switch from activating in response to the door's movement. Gene made another adjustment to the wiring, and the system's motion detectors were turned around to watch the walls instead of the room. He dealt with the building's security cameras by catching their UHF channels and replaying an hour-long segment of the camera recordings from the same time the night before. *One hour of empty hallways should cover their tracks*, he thought, *assuming any of the security personnel were even awake and monitoring the cameras.*

With the alarm system effectively disabled, the pair entered the building, and Tony led the way straight to the safe. Having done his advance research well, Gene was prepared. He drilled a small hole in the safe and inserted a mini-camera in the shape of a wire. This let him see the reset button inside the safe, so he pressed it with a special robotic wire. With the safe open, they scooped the piles of cash into the bags they'd brought with them and shut the safe, which was left waiting for a new reset code. "There's no time," said Gene.

They headed back to the side door, reset and re-activated the alarm, then exited the building. It would be days before Tony's "rival gang" even knew they'd been robbed.

The two left the scene of the crime feeling mighty satisfied with themselves. After splitting the cash, they exchanged thumbs-up and high- fives before going their separate ways. Gene had plans to go car shopping with his take. Tony was thinking about treating a certain blond lady to a romantic evening like no other. He smiled as he recalled her sultry voice telling him to get a good car for making love.

They were both thinking about future capers, now that this one had gone so well. Too bad they forgot to factor in the fickle nature of Lady Luck.

Chapter 5

Romancing Lady Luck

Tony was not in a good mood. Charlene had blown him off once again. Since she'd taken that job at the ad agency—her first since graduating—she didn't have as much time for him. And besides, he was now competing for her attention with the handsome models and other guys she worked with. Damn, he was not used to this!

It was going to take some work to get her attention on him again, but that was okay. He had a plan. If he needed to make an appointment to get his foot in the door, he'd make an appointment.

"C'mere, Silvano. I need you to make a phone call for me." Tony handed the cell phone to his pal. "Charlene won't talk to me, so pretend you're calling from the Furniture Emporium, that big fancy store that just opened."

"And then what?" asked Silvano.

"Find out about her. Who books her appointments? Say that she's just right for our new ad campaign."

"Boss, we don't advertise—"

"Not us, you idiot—the Furniture Emporium! That's who you're pretending to be, remember?"

Silvano took the phone and dialed the number. "Good day, I'm calling from the Furniture Emporium," he said with a mocking smile. "We're looking at starting a new ad campaign."

"Oh yes, sir, you've called the right place!" came the breathy voice of the receptionist. "How may I help you?"

"We've been seeing your new model, Charlene Palmer, on TV and hearing a lot about her. She seems perfect for our new campaign. Could you tell us who handles her booking?"

"Of course, sir. Yes, she is in quite a lot demand, but I believe she still has the rest of the week free. Shall I transfer you to her desk?"

"I would like to personally arrange an appointment with her, thank you."

"Of course. She insists on personal involvement with all her clients. I'm sure you will find her entirely satisfactory."

"I'm sure we will. Thank you again." Silvano hung up the phone. "Geez, Tony. If I do any more of these jobs for you, I'll turn three shades whiter and start acting like I graduated, or something!"

***

Tony and Silvano entered the Furniture Emporium and gazed in fascination at the ultra-modern decor around them. Achromatic glass walls and bluish plastic.fixtures set off the splashes of hot color that formed a signature palette for the pricey furnishings arranged in tasteful display throughout the ground floor. Flanking the entryway were two couches styled like ladies' shoes, with reading lamps supported by the "spike heels" done in shiny red plastic. Red velvet seating areas made up the "toe" of the shoes.

"Wow, look at that," marveled Silvano, tightly clutching the briefcase that contained Tony's spending money. "Seven-foot-long shoes for your relaxing pleasure!"

"Charlene will love those," smiled Tony. "Women always fall for shoes. That's like orgasm number-one for the ladies."

A mousy-looking female employee of the store approached them tentatively. "Where's the manager?" snapped Tony.

"You'll find him on the second floor, right this way," said the employee, gesturing towards an escalator that rose between ranks of elegant dining tables on one side, and comfortable loungers on the other.

The two schemers went up the escalator and walked across another large showroom decorated as if it were the living room of a posh penthouse apartment. Tony stared appreciatively at a plush, oversized sofa. It was upholstered in soft leather of a buttery-yellow color and lit from overhead with electrical plasma balls. *Sex must be really good on this sofa,* thought Tony.

"Welcome to Furniture Emporium," said the manager. Alerted by his employee, he'd come out to greet them and to make sure nothing that wasn't nailed down walked out with them. "How may I help you?"

Tony stared down from his height at the slight man. "You are the manager?"

"Of course."

"Let's get right to the point, my fancy guy, nicely dressed with a little tie." The manager's face reddened, but his salesroom-perfected smile didn't slip. "I want to rent this building for the next two days. How much?"

"Oh, sir, you must be joking? Ha ha, that is funny."

"I'm quite serious."

"Seriously? I'm afraid I don't have an answer for you right now. These kinds of offers don't come along very often, ha ha—"

"I *said* I am quite serious."

"Of course. I would have to think about it for a bit . . ."

"Look," said Tony, "you can't afford this thinking because you could be in trouble with us!"

"Sir, there is no need to raise your tone with me! Do I have to call security?"

"Five hundred thousand dollars! That's how serious I am!"

"Hmm, so that's one million for two days—"

"No, I said exactly five hundred thousand. For two days."

"Oh, very well. In that case . . . promise you won't break anything . . . or tear the place up!"

"I'll take that as a yes! We got a deal, fag—you don't mind if I call you that, do you?" Tony extracted some bundles of cash from the briefcase Silvano held. He tossed the stacks at the manager's feet. "Consider that my deposit. We'll be here first thing in the morning to begin our rental." He gestured to Silvano and turned to go.

"Um, sir, perhaps we should sign a contract," the manager ventured.

Tony turned to glare at him while Silvano sneered.

"Thank you, sir. It's a pleasure doing business with you." Shaking, the manager picked up the stacks of cash and hurried with them into his office.

Riding the down escalator, Silvano asked Tony, "So how are we going to get all that money back?"

Tony shrugged and grinned. "Maybe we'll win the lottery."

***

Charlene strode into the Furniture Emporium like a woman on a mission. She was smartly dressed in a skirt-suit that was very nearly the same deep scarlet as the shoe-sofas that flanked the front door. A store clerk met her and announced that her appointment was waiting for her at the top of the escalator. She rode to the second floor and walked through the showroom, stopping to run her hand over the buttery-soft leather that covered an oversized yellow sofa.

Through the open door to the manager's office, she caught a glimpse of a man's size-11 feet crossed on top of the huge walnut desk. The feet were wearing polished loafers of brown Italian leather. Those shoes, she recognized.

"Hey, what is this—some kind of a joke?"

Tony lifted his legs off the desk and swiveled in the chair to put his feet on the floor, and then stood up and came towards her. All in one smooth motion.

"Hello, dear Charlene. I'm sorry I didn't buy you a flower. Instead, I'm buying an advertisement."

"Oh, swell. What kind of story are we telling? The college grad who nearly dropped out, and now he's the world's greatest furniture salesman. Is that it?"

"Yeah, yeah. It's rare that you meet a man who can climb this far in just one night, isn't it?"

"You absolutely amaze me, Tony. I'm speechless." She set down her briefcase and checked her hair in the small mirror she pulled from her purse. "All right, let's talk business."

"Okay, let me show you around the place." He took her arm and led her over to the yellow couch. "I saw you admiring this finely crafted piece. Does it give you any ideas?"

"It really is sensational. It would make a great backdrop for your ad." She tapped the side of her cheek as she was thinking. "How about this: the owner of the furniture house, the boss of the place, is sitting at this beautiful yellow couch, and suddenly two female clerks are bringing him his morning coffee and telling him very good news . . ."

Tony struck a dignified pose, for a moment, then started to laugh. "He accidentally walks into the couch, gets crazy about it, yells, and two guys come up and pick it up, then throw it out a window! What do you think?"

Charlene blinked, then went along with the game. "And the couch falls on some grandma's head, and it ends with him in jail, maybe?"

"That's right! Well, maybe with a happier ending. Some stray finds it and likes it. It becomes a nice, warm new home." He winked to her. "You are not going to win, you know."

"You're good. I won't argue with you. Let's do a night shot on this. I'll come back with my team, and we will make something that is positively delicious!"

"I'm all yours," said Tony, walking her back to his desk, where she'd left her purse and briefcase. She gathered up her belongings and turned to leave.

"What about dinner?" he asked.

She turned back to him, looking him over with her pretty eyes. "You're asking me for a date? Fine. Meet me at Paradiso Restaurant. Nine thirty. Don't be late."

Chapter 6
Lady Luck Flies Away

Huddled in Gene's cramped, stuffy garage, Tony watched Gene proudly detailing his new car. The red BMW 850 gleamed under the shop lights that hung from the ceiling. Gene took out the ECU and the chip. Then he connected it to the computer and altered the engine map.

"Tuning done. I think this is the most I've ever re-mapped a chip!" Gene said to no one in particular, though his voice brimmed with satisfaction. "She can roar like a lion, or purr like a kitten—it's all in the programming."

"So how much tax do you have to pay for the extra engine displacement?" asked Tony.

"Not that much. They don't know it has six hundred-plus horsepower, instead of the standard three hundred seventy-five."

"Ha, you screwed them! I guess they never saw a car like this outside of a museum." Tony grinned at the look of satisfaction on Gene's face. He drew a roll of bills from his pocket and peeled off a few to show to Gene. "Say, I need to borrow this car for a couple of days . . ."

"What?!" exclaimed Gene.

"I got some important meetings lined up. Here's a grand—"

"A grand! That won't even cover the damage if you mess it up. And besides, don't you have a car?"

Tony shrugged. "Mine needs a tune-up and some body work on the front end. I need something right now that will impress my contacts. All right, here's ten grand, take it or leave it."

Gene reluctantly accepted the cash. The way he'd been spending lately, there wasn't much left from his share of the capers they'd been doing lately. Tony let Gene know there'd be more jobs for him in the future, assuming he played his part well now.

Gene handed over the keys and watched as Tony roared out of the garage.

"You better bring it back with a full tank!" he shouted into the air.

***

Soft lights and polished wood lent a soothing ambiance to the restaurant where Tony and Charlene were making small talk over pre-dinner drinks. For once, she was focusing on him as if he were the only person in her universe. She'd already been surprised when she walked in five minutes earlier and found him waiting for her at the best table in the dining room. And she'd looked for his car in the parking lot, too.

The waiter served their entrees and poured the wine. As they tasted the savory food, Charlene beamed at Tony. He felt as if she'd thrown out golden lines between the two of them. "Mmm, excellent," he said. "Haven't had a meal like this in ages!"

She cut her food in tiny pieces and nibbled at them delicately. With the grace of a princess, she took the napkin and dabbed at the corner of her lip.

"Why must you cut your food into such tiny pieces?" asked Tony, teasing her.

Charlene ignored him. "So, what TV networks would you like to advertise your Furniture Emporium?" she asked.

"What do I know? I'll leave you to manage that. If you ask me, I'd say only sports channels."

"You've got the major networks like NBC and cable like CNN. Those networks also have corporate co-sponsors. Everything depends on how much money you have in your pocket."

"Money is not a problem. I want a full package. You?"

"It can cost from one hundred thousand dollars to two hundred thousand dollars a week."

"That's okay with me. I like the way you are working. You are like your job . . ."

She blushed and looked down at the table. "Let's just say I'm lucky to be working the job of my dreams."

After more small talk, the end of the evening arrived. Tony looked into her eyes. "I am not sure what is better: to be working with you or to be hung up on you . . ."

She folded her napkin, looked away, and then looked back again. "It's been a nice evening. Thank you for the lovely dinner."

"So, you have positive vibrations?"

"Oh, definitely yes! There is something in you. Something fast, movable. I don't know yet what . . ."

"But you are going to find out," he stated with a charming smile.

"Yes."

He stood and went around the table to help her by pulling back her chair as she rose. "Why don't we start with another tour of the Furniture Emporium?" he asked as he helped her on with her coat. "I have many more things to show you."   .

***

Only a few spotlights on selected displays penetrated the dim lighting of the Furniture Emporium at night. Charlene and Tony walked through the ground floor to the escalator. It was silenced for the night, so they walked up to the showroom with the yellow sofa. "Just the two of us," he smiled.

"Um. Shall we get down to business?"

"Right. You should wear something in yellow, so that you really match the couch."

"Yeah, sure. Okay, let's do a dry run before we film tomorrow. Tony, you are sitting in the middle, and two beautiful ladies will bring you coffee. One from the one side and one from the other."

Tony shook his head. "It will be better if I am sitting here on the couch like a boss, and you, a very recognizable face in advertising, come to me and say: 'Only the best for the best. You are the star!'"

Charlene considered this. "Not a bad idea. Well, we can try several different combinations, then we will see." She looked in the mirror on the display wall over the couch and touched up her lipstick. "Oh, I'm all red in the face! Okay, here goes."

She pushed Tony into his place on the yellow sofa. "Action! Good day, my valued customers. We are here at Furniture Emporium, the biggest and best furniture showroom around! Next to me is the owner, Tony Donatelli. Tony, the customers want to know why you have chosen this station to carry your message." She walked around the couch to stand behind Tony and put one hand on his shoulder. With the other hand, she stroked the couch.

"Only the best for the best!" he asserted, beaming into the imaginary camera.

Still behind him, Charlene clapped her hands. "Bring us the coffee," she ordered the imaginary clerks standing to the side of the imaginary stage.

Tony jumped as if his heart stopped, but then he laughed. "You frightened me with that little twist."

"What can I say? I'm a bad cat." She grinned.

Tony stood up and faced her. He beckoned with his finger. "Come with me. I've got to show you something."

He grabbed her hand and pulled her behind a tinted glass wall. Leaning in very close, with his eyes lusting, he pushed her into the wall. "You really think that I am the right guy for TV?"

"Hmm . . ."

"If I'm not, tell me now . . ." And he moved to kiss her. He put his hands on the wall, one on either side of her, pinning her in. He first gave her a slow kiss just to see her reaction, then started to give her a strong, loving one.

Charlene turned her head to the side. "Is this part of my payment for the advertisement?"

"Your check is on the table," he answered. "Do whatever you want with it." He waited till she turned back to him, then completed his kiss.

Games with women . . ., Tony mused as they silently slid deeper into the kisses and caresses that foretold lovemaking. *I will give to you, I will not give to you. Why can't it be simple and easy? She must give to me on the end. I know that every woman is like a stone tower. But this is not how you play with Tony.*

Having finally broken the ice with a kiss, Tony suggested they return to the yellow couch for a more comfortable experience. The smooth leather fairly glowed under the soft purple halogen lights of the display room. The couch was big enough for the two of them to stretch out side-by-side.

"Mmm, I like this place. You can practically smell the modernity," sighed Charlene.

Furniture was the last thing on Tony's mind. Moving down so his head was at the level of her navel, he started to tickle and kiss her.

"Stop, Tony . . ."

"Don't cha wanna have a boy like me . . . " he sang it in a little voice. "You know that song?"

"Don't cha wanna have a freak like me?" she laughed back.

"Mmm, I like that song. I like you. I've got to draw you: I love you with my tongue on your pretty navel."

She pushed his head from her, but he grabbed her around the back. He slid her panties down over her knees. With his fingernails, he traced the lines of her tattoo, which encircled her bottom like a tanga. Then, like a tiger, he turned her to her front side and continued to draw a heart with his nails.

"You are a nasty cat. Who would believe it?" he murmured.

"You don't know anything yet," she answered.

"I doubt that. All princesses are masked with a big scarf." He kissed her very deep before the moment passed, but she pushed him away.

"Do I need to have experience to have a good taste?" she asked.

"Nice words. You are killing me." He shut her up with another kiss.

On the wall of the Furniture Emporium, a large clock above the yellow sofa ticked its way towards midnight.

"It's nice making love at midnight, isn't it?" asked Tony.

"Mmm. You think we should count it . . . down? Nine, eight . . ." breathed Charlene.

"Seven, six—" Tony stopped abruptly and stood up. "Ah, I hate these chains and watches around my head and hands."

"Let me handle it. You keep counting." Charlene began removing his watch and neck chain.

"Nasty. Five, four . . ."

"Good watch. A Daytona Rolex!" Charlene exclaimed.

"Is it the original?"

"No, it's a copy, fake guy. You are the original." She pushed him back down on the couch and unfastened the rest of his clothing. With clothing strewn everywhere across the couch, they made wild love and together counted towards their climax: "Three, two, one . . ."

***

Midnight had come and gone. Charlene declared that, as she had to go to work in the morning, it was time to call it a night. She gathered her clothes and dressed herself. Tony did the same. Always the perfect gentleman—at least when he remembered to be—he walked her out into the parking lot where their cars stood side-by-side. The red BMW gleamed under the tall overhead lights.

Charlene looked with admiration at the magnificent vehicle. "You know, before I leave, I'd like to just sit in that beauty for a while," she said, smiling up at him.

Tony unlocked the door for her and went around to sit on the driver's side. He lit a cigarette and offered her one, then lit hers. They smoked and talked for a while, about everything and nothing.

"What color of eyes do you have?" she asked.

"You see everything, don't you?" he said. "My eyes are hazel: The outer circle is brown; the inner circle is green. A twist mixture."

"When I look at you from the side, they're dark; but when you come closer, they are green. The brown is a noble color, and the green sets off those who like to discover new things." She smiled.

"Far different from your cold, icy eyes."

Charlene laughed. "I should go. It's getting really late."

Tony put his arm around her and kissed her. She looked him in the eyes.

"You worked me out. You totally rocked me this time."

Their kisses grew deeper. Soon they were writhing together passionately, and Charlene dropped her panties again.

***

Their evening was about to turn into a night when Charlene pointed out the lateness of the hour in a tone that allowed no argument. Tony walked her once more to her car, opened the door for her, and saw her safely inside.

"Feels like a letdown after being in your luxury beast," she smiled through the open window. She put the key in the ignition, started the car, then glanced up at him as he stood in the darkness and looked down at her.

"We could do it again," he said. "No need to wait so long this time."

"I don't know. But I don't know how this is going to finish, either." With her foot on the brake, she engaged the gear shift. "You see," she said, looking back at him one more time, "I'm moving to California next week. I have a chance to work in the movies. It's been my dream . . . I hope you'll understand."

"What?!!!"

"Don't be so upset. I'll write. And we could still visit each other— the world has airplanes, you know. And besides, I threw the dart, so you know I'll be back in your life again." She started to raise the window, but Tony reached his hand in to stop it. "I don't want you to do this—you can't go!" He was shouting now.

"Cut it out, Tony. You're being a pig! Good-bye!" She slapped his hand away and closed the window. Stepping on the gas, she sped away without a backward glance. Tony was just barely able to jerk his hand clear of the window as he watched his girl disappear into the night.

"Arrgggghhh!" he screamed into the empty space around him. Furious, he turned back to the BMW and slammed his fist into the driver's door. The pain brought tears to his eyes as the signet ring he wore cut into his fingers with the impact.

Shaking his hand, he threw the door open, got in the car, and roared out of the parking lot.

Chapter 7
Lottery Heist

W eeks turned into months, and months into years, but there was no word from Charlene. Tony went on with his life, establishing businesses to keep busy and forget about Charlene.

"Another boring day in paradise," Gene announced as he signed in for another day of work at Tony's garage/gas station/chop shop.

"Are you missing your exciting life in the joint?" asked Tony.

Gene wasn't listening. His attention was on the TV that was broadcasting the winning lottery numbers, and his face changed from bored to excited. "Fuck! Look at that! Some lucky bastard won $20 million. This is a game worth playing!" Gene exclaimed.

"Or tampering with," said Tony.

Just then a red BMW 850CSi convertible screamed into the parking lot and halted in front of the gas pumps.

"Astonishing," said Tony.

"Amazing," said Gene. "That car doesn't exist as a convertible."

"It must be someone's off-series production," answered Tony. "Whoa, so is the driver!"

An elegantly dressed blond woman exited the car, flashing her long legs as she gracefully unfolded herself from the low-slung driver's seat.

"I'll take you to the candy shop," Tony sang in a low voice. The two men watched the women saunter towards them into the gas station office, each keeping to himself the moment of recognition: this was either the long-lost Charlene, or someone who looked and moved exactly like her.

She walked into the station like she owned the place. The two men stared as she twirled around to examine the candy section. After selecting a chocolate bar, she held it up. "This, please. And could you fill up my tank . . . Tony." Slowly, she smiled and turned to walk back to her car.

Tony looked at Gene. "Go fill the lady's tank. You know more about these high-performance cars." Then he turned back to Charlene. "Long time no see. What brings you to these parts?"

"I got tired of LA," she answered with a shrug. "I missed the seasons, so I decided to move back here."

"Yeah, where did this one-of-a-kind convertible come from?" asked Gene. He'd just finished gassing up her car and was cleaning the windshield for good measure.

"I'm filming an ad for the State Lottery. This car is the bonus prize for the lucky winner." She smiled. "The director called a halt to the shooting, some technical problem or other, so I decided to borrow her and go for spin. We're just down the road near the bridge."

"Hmmmm. So you're with the State Lottery, huh?" said Tony, an idea forming in his head.

"In case you didn't know, I'm the new face for the State Lottery." She got into the car and slammed the door. Tony recovered his wits enough to ask her, "Uhh . . . that will be seventy dollars, please?"

Charlene tapped the gas pedal a couple of times to check the gauge, then opened her purse and pulled out a thick wad of hundred dollar bills. She peeled off a bill and threw it at Tony. "Here!"

She put the car in gear and drove off, almost running Tony over.

"Sorryyy!" Charlene's voice trailed off as she spun out of the lot.

"Fuck, that blonde almost ran me over!" he cried.

Gene laughed. "Ooh, she is good. Dangerous. She needs to be caught."

Tony looked at the hundred-dollar bill in his hand. Charlene had written her phone number in the margin.

***

Later that evening, Tony and Charlene took the car for a drive. Charlene was at the wheel. The fast-pumping beat of an early-'90s techno hit played over the stereo system, until she said, "Sorry, no disco anymore." It had been a fitting background for Charlene's rapid acceleration when they reached open highway. Driving fast and changing gears, she soon pushed the speedometer to 155 mph.

"Top speed, baby!" Tony beamed.

"Why can't we go faster?" Charlene was leaning forward in the driver's seat, her breath coming short and fast, a flush of excitement on her cheeks.

"It has a governor to limit the speed."

"Take it off!" Charlene demanded.

"No way!" Tony went on to explain, "One hundred fifty-five miles per hour is a piece of cake, but more than that and you feel like the car wants to take off at every turn. Every bend becomes a right angle, your braking distance exceeds one hundred fifty miles, which means that if something is blocking your way three hundred miles in front of you, you're dead because you'll crash into it at over sixty miles per hour. Your brain cannot cope with the impact, and you'll get tunnel vision. But practice can reduce that. And no one—absolutely no one—expects you to go that fast."

"What about the brakes?" asked Charlene.

Tony put his head in his hands. "Just don't, please don't."

"Why, am I scaring you? I need to practice."

"Practice at one hundred fifty-five miles per hour? That's not a good idea."

She started to brake, using the tactic of pressing the brake pedal in pulses.

"Yeeeessss, stop! Stop now!" shouted Tony.

As the speed began to drop, Charlene pressed the brake pedal to the maximum. Tony hit the windshield. *Not again,* thought Tony. *This is not my lucky moment.*

"Hmm, the disks must be hot," observed Charlene. She put the car in gear, pressed the gas pedal, and drove on—keeping to the speed limit for a change.

Charlene drove for a while, then pulled off and parked at an overlook. No one else was around. They got out of the car and watched the city lights for a while. Charlene had been leaning back against the hood of the car; she wiggled her bottom backwards until she was sitting on it. She opened her legs and brought Tony closer into a hug. They kissed and writhed together. Then he drew back and said, "I want to do it inside the lottery building."

***

Charlene used her ID card to let them into the lottery headquarters building.

Hmmmm. Easy access, Tony thought. "So where's the studio used for the lottery draw?" Tony asked Charlene.

"There," Charlene said, pointing to a big door nearby. "And that's where the balls are kept."

They went through the darkened hallway to find an empty office. With the door closed, Tony started to pick up where they left off, with lots of kissing and . . .

He lowered his head to the same level as her navel, then started to tickle and kiss her."

"Stop, Tony!" she said.

"I like you. I can't help being drawn to you. I love tasting you and kissing your pretty navel."

He grabbed Charlene around the back, took her dress off, and let it drop. He remembered the tattoo around her bottom; now it had been enhanced with flowers and vines curling over the inked lines. He traced the tattoo with his finger. "I see you're still a dirty girl."

"You don't know anything yet," she answered.

"I doubt that. All princesses wear masks." He kissed her deeply.

"Do I need to have experience to have good taste?" she asked when the kiss ended.

"Nice words," he remarked. "You're killing me; stop it. Your voice is hot enough."

She shut him up with a kiss. On the wall, a large clock indicated a few minutes before midnight. Tony stopped his attention to her and exclaimed, "Ah, I hate having these chains and watches around my neck and wrists."

"Let me handle it." She began removing his accessories one by one.

"Sexy," he said appreciatively.

She took his watch off. He moved her backwards, so she was sitting on the desk with her legs spread. As she positioned herself, her right hand knocked over a souvenir container of Power Balls that was sitting on the desk behind her. The balls flowed over the desk and bounced onto the floor.

Tony entered her, and they began moving rhythmically together, slowly at first, then harder and faster.

***

Back at the gas station, Gene was his usual melancholic self. Tony arrived and asked, "Are you ready to be a lottery millionaire?"

"What?" a confused Gene asked.

"Come with me. Let me show you something." The two went out and drove off.

They arrived at a shopping mall and went to the rooftop. Gene and Tony stared out at the lottery headquarters building across the street. The sleek glass-and-steel monolith soared up into the bright sky. Above the gaping entrance was an illuminated sign that flashed its message: WELCOME TO OUR STATE — PLAY OUR LOTTO — THE POWER BALL, AND WIN MEGA MILLIONS!

"There!" Tony declared, with arms wide open as if to introduce the prize to be won.

"I do buy lottery tickets—we sell them at the gas station, you know that, right?—but how many lifetimes do I need before I hit the jackpot? A person's odds of winning the jackpot are one in one hundred seventy-five million."

"Unless you control the number combinations," said Tony.

With that, Gene's eyes beamed like a newly installed headlight. "Yes! Why haven't I thought of that?"

"That's what you get for sniffing gasoline," joked Tony.

A serious-looking Gene ignored the gibe and started thinking of a way to get into the lottery building.

For days, Gene studied the lottery building's detailed floor plan after hacking into a database. He got inside the building by joining a group of foreigners given a tour of the place. In that way, it was easy for him to take some pictures and videos.

As the end of the week approached, Gene and Tony went back to the rooftop of the shopping mall.

"They still use analog cameras. All we need to do is take the tapes out," said Gene.

"I have a better idea. If they catch us, I'll blow up all the columns that keep this building standing," said Tony. "There should be no evidence against us."

"And how are you going to do that?"

"You're gonna do it, you expert," said Tony.

"We need access. There are a lot of people outside; we can't break in without making a sound. Charlene's got some lottery connections . . . Maybe we can—"

"Nah, I don't want to involve her," Tony interrupted Gene before he could finish his suggestion. He was deep in thought and was observing people on the street below. From his vantage point, he could also see through the windows of the offices in the lottery building. With his binoculars, he saw one man carrying a tray of what looked like ping pong balls. When the man turned his back, Tony read something on the back of the man's shirt: "Johnson."

***

The next day, while Gene was busy preparing the explosives and other devices, Tony went to Mr. Johnson's house in the guise of a salesman.

"Good day. Are you interested in seeing the latest household machines for the upcoming year?" Intrigued, Mr. Johnson invited him in.

Tony went on, "Oh yes, you see, I am not like the others; you don't have to sign anything. I just need your data in order to put you on the list of our potential buyers. You will become a member and will have discounts on our products. The more you buy, the more discounts you get!" He chuckled. "We are giving prizes, too! You can have an Internet account and a starter kit to build your own pyramid scheme, the 'Eight-Ball' model. The scheme requires a person to recruit two others, who must each recruit two others, who must each recruit two others. It will be very profitable."

Mr. Johnson looked at some catalogues Tony had given him. "This is great! My wife likes buying from catalogs."

Tony gave him a sign-up form. "Write down your address here, and don't forget to add the information about your ID. In fact, just give me your ID card, so you don't make a mistake."

Mr. Johnson retrieved his ID from his jacket pocket, then gave it to Tony.

"Excellent! It will just take a minute!" Tony took the ID and pretended to fill in the forms. He put the ID into a device that looked like a calculator, but was actually made to clone identity cards.

"It's done!" said Tony. "You see how quick, safe, and easy it is in this new Internet era. Everything is all set."

Tony handed back the ID card to the old man and left. "Okay. Thanks again for your time, Mr. Johnson. I will say good-bye now because I have to continue sales with the rest of your neighborhood."

* * *

Under the cover of the night, Tony and Gene got inside the lottery building using the cloned ID card. Gene bypassed video signals to the CCTV. With his tools and expertise, Gene opened the vault containing the briefcases holding the balls. Gene donned and stretched a pair of gloves over his hand. He carefully took five white balls and a red one and placed them in a smaller briefcase.

"Are we done?" Tony asked.

"Not yet! I have to finish installing the explosives. I suppose you can help me with that," said Gene. "Hide them well. We don't know yet when we'll actually blow this up. I'll use my cell phone to trigger these babies."

They left the place before the break of dawn, removing traces of the break-in on their way out.

The following day was spent tampering with the balls. Tony got a lottery ticket; the number combination was based on the numbers on the stolen balls. Gene started working on the balls. He was like a scientist working in his lab, while Tony was like a dog sleeping in his bed.

As night fell, Gene returned to the lottery building to make the switch, just in time for the lottery draw the next day.

***

Charlene was announcing the game from inside the lottery building. She pressed the switch, and the balls began to rotate. "The first number is two!"

Tony watched the lottery draw on the TV at his workshop. "Here it goes!"

On the TV, Charlene smiled and took out the second ball. "The second number is four!"

"Yes!" said Tony. He looked at the wall above the TV, where a combination had been written in big numbers: "2 4 9 33 23 39." And those were the winning numbers!

"Twenty million!" Tony pumped his fist.

After claiming the prize, Tony deposited the check into his bank account. Gene had to wait for the check to clear before getting his share.

However, Lady Luck had other plans. After a few days, Charlene drove into the gas station lot. She was looking for Tony. "They know about the scam," she said.

"What scam?" asked Tony, trying to look innocent.

"Police have been questioning the workers at the lottery building. I overheard one of the investigators mentioning your name."

"How did they get the trace?" he asked.

"They do not check the tapes until something happens. The balls were discovered to have been tampered with. You may have perfectly tampered with the balls, but not all of the cameras. They are still reviewing the tapes and access logs. No final findings yet."

She looked at him and shook her head. "To become a big gambler, you must be a small gambler first. I think you should know that," said Charlene as she got in her car and drove off.

Tony phoned Gene. "We're screwed! We need to destroy evidence."

Then Tony heard the police siren. "The cops are here! Let's meet at the shopping mall. We need to get rid of the evidence." He ran out the backdoor and sped away, but the cops spotted him and gave chase.

Tony drove down a one-way road. He floored the pedal and entered a roundabout curve. The speed sign showed "MAX 55 mph"! His Alfa Romeo 164 passed the cars on the right at twice that speed. Now, Tony was out of the roundabout. A tunnel appeared in the distance. He looked in the rearview mirror, dropped his speed, and entered the lane diagonally from the opposite direction.

The cops lost him.

***

The dark night was lit up for the street festival going on in the area between the lottery building and the shopping mall. Caught in the traffic jam on the way to the shopping mall, Tony braked in the middle of the street and got out of the car. Running through the traffic and dodging the crowds, Tony saw Gene walking fast towards the shopping mall entrance. He caught up with him and pointed to the access stairs to the roof. Gene nodded, and they went up together.

Officer Brian Scofield saw Tony and Gene heading to the top of the shopping mall building and alerted the other cops. The police cars arrived. Brian and his partner, Dave Wychowski, ran into the mall, pushing everybody out of the way, and got into the elevator just as the doors were closing.

"Does this lift go to the very top?" asked Brian, addressing the passengers who were staring at the cops.

"Yes, sir, it goes straight to the top," answered one of the elevator passengers. "Nice views out there. Too bad you can't climb the tower. There's gonna be fireworks soon."

The glass windows of the elevator shaft revealed the brightly lit tower of the lottery headquarters. The elevator filled with "oohs" and "ahhs" from its passengers. "Look! The tower. Beautiful!" said one.

Brian turned to Dave. "Lucky us, this elevator moves too slow. Fuck, I don't care about the damn fireworks."

The elevator stopped at the top floor of the shopping mall, and Brian and Dave got out onto a floor filled with people having a party. Brian pushed people out of the way, and he and Dave bounded up the emergency stairs to the roof, only to be halted at the red exit door. It was locked. They tried kicking the door; it didn't budge.

"Fuck! Are we going to wait for the manager to come and open the door?" said Brian, waving his hands in a gesture of disgust.

Dave took his gun out of its holster and shot the lock. The door popped open, and they raced up the stairs.

***

Gene and Tony were just about to ascend into the maintenance area below the roof when the two cops burst out of the emergency stairs. Tony, who was trailing behind Gene, retreated and ran the other way, but Gene's foot got stuck in one of the gaps in the stairs.

Tony saw it, but he continued to run. He slipped through a maintenance access.

The policemen caught up with Gene. "Stop! Police! Hands up!" said Officer Brian. "Gene Nielsen? You're under arrest! You have the right to remain silent. Anything you say can and will be used against you . . ."

Officer Dave went behind Gene, yanked his arms behind his back, and snapped on a pair of handcuffs.

"You think you can escape?" said Brian, menacingly.

The cops headed down the stairs and out of the mall with Gene in custody. He grimaced, knowing he would spend a very long time in jail for this one. Reporters who were covering the street festival got wind of the incident. They rushed to interview Gene and the arresting officers.

One of the officers shoved Gene into the backseat of the police car.

While the officers were fielding questions from the reporters, Gene reached for his cell phone in his back pocket, but he hesitated. *Not now.*

I'm too near. The impact is going to hit me, Gene thought while turning his head to survey the lottery building, *and Charlene!*

The crowd thickened, and Gene could no longer see Charlene, who was talking to reporters at the lottery building's ground floor.

***

From afar, Tony was watching Gene as he was escorted by the policemen. He also saw Charlene being interviewed. Tony knew Gene could detonate the explosives anytime soon. His phone rang. "Boss, we're here. Rooftop of the mall," said the caller.

"Transfer to the lottery building rooftop," ordered Tony.

Tony ran across the street, blended in with the crowd, and entered the lottery building. He saw Charlene and approached her. "Hurry up, the whole building is going to blow up," whispered Tony.

"What?" asked a surprised Charlene. "Who will—?"

"Gene! We're running out of time. There's a helicopter on the rooftop. Let's go!" Charlene took Tony by the hand, and they both started running. Gene saw them as they were making their way up the stairs.

***

Feeling abandoned, Gene was overcome with rage. He recalled one specific moment, when he was fixing his car after Tony had demanded to use it, so he could impress some important contacts. He was checking in and around the passenger's seat when his fingers closed on a wisp of slippery fabric. He pulled out a pair of pink women's panties from beneath the seat. *What the fuck?* he thought, holding them up to the light. Embroidered on the left hip were the initials "CP"—Charlene Palmer, the cold and beautiful blond goddess of his secret dreams.

Gene's musings were interrupted by the sound of the car doors opening. Officers Brian and Dave were all set to take him to the police station.

As the police car left the area, music started to play on the shopping mall roof as thousands of different lights flashed in the sky.

Upon reaching the next block, Gene had to make a decision: *You abandoned me! If I can't have her, neither can you!* Gene pressed his cell phone's call button, triggering the explosives tied to the lottery building's pillars. A big explosion detonated, and the building crashed down like dominoes, leaving nothing but a big dust cloud surrounded by fireworks.

Chapter 8
The Genius and Pete

The morning sun shone brightly on the rectangle of packed earth that formed the prison exercise yard. Gene completed his daily three laps around the yard. Most of his fellow inmates had gathered at the picnic tables to smoke and shoot the shit until the bell rang that signaled the end of the exercise period and the return to the prison interior for the day. Not Gene. He jogged over to his preferred corner, the spot in the exercise yard he now thought of as "his," and he began working through the calisthenics series he'd put together from online instructional videos he had accessed in the prison library.

In the few months since the prison doors had clanged behind him, he'd come to accept his situation. It wasn't so bad, really. With his technical knowledge and the ingratiating manner he'd adopted as a matter of survival, he was soon getting special treatment from the warden and prison staff. His position as trustee gave him access to all the important places—the library, the computer lab, the metal shop, even the commissary. From here, he could dispense favors to the other inmates, making him invaluable to the various gang leaders inside the prison. Being an equal-opportunity benefactor, Gene was able to insulate himself from much of the inter-gang conflict that simmered like a slow boil beneath the surface of the inmates' daily activities.

Release day finally came. The prison psychiatrist looked through his file as Gene sat stiffly in the chair by the desk, feeling uncomfortable in the cheap suit he wore in place of the prison jumpsuit he'd grown accustomed to. The shrink put down the papers and looked at Gene.

"Well, Genius . . . any regrets?"

Gene just gave him a sly smile.

***

Gene stirred in his sleep. *He was making love to Charlene, thrusting harder and faster until he came. Stars exploded behind his closed eyelids at the exquisite feeling, as if in a dream . . .*

It *was* a dream, unfortunately. Gene woke up just then, alone in his narrow bed in the cheap apartment he was renting. For a few moments, he tried to sink back into sleep and capture the feeling once more. That didn't work, so he threw back the covers and got to his feet. Noticing the faint dawn light peeking around the edge of the window shades, he gave up. Early as it was, he wouldn't go back to sleep. He went to the kitchen to make some coffee.

"She should have been mine! Fuck, damn it!" Gene swore. Sitting at the little table, he sipped the strong coffee. It tasted as bitter as his thoughts. "After being like a submissive dog around that jerk, he left me high and dry! He didn't give me my share of the twenty million. Good thing he died in the explosion. My only regret is that the idiot had Charlene with him."

Fortunately, Gene had saved for a rainy day. Before he'd gone into prison, Gene had hidden his wealth: the kilo of gold he'd purchased for 50,000 dollars and some cash. He'd cleverly buried them in a vacant lot near his old apartment. No one would take them from there, he'd thought. And it was true. The gold and cash were right where he'd left it. He took the gold to the buyers, and he sold it for 50,000 dollars. *The same price I paid for it,* he thought. *Gold always keeps its value.*

***

While out on the street one day, Gene saw two thieves breaking into a car, a Jaguar. One guy was holding some kind of a decoder remote; it looked like a TV remote control. He hit a button on the remote, and the Jaguar opened with a *beep.*

This intrigued Gene, who was hungry for more information on the latest technology and trends after serving his jail term. He read about them while in jail, but real-world application was impossible. *I need to get my hands on that device and reverse-engineer it.*

Gene stopped and opened his newspaper, as if to scan the day's headlines. He walked on nonchalantly, pretending to be interested in anything but the scene at the car. Then, when he got to the car's rear, he scribbled "CARTER" in the margin of the newspaper. He then got in his car and waited for them to finish hotwiring the Jaguar. One guy got a license plate from his bag and replaced the Jaguar's "CARTER" license plate with it.

Gene followed them. The Jaguar parked right behind another car. From a safe distance, Gene was watching. The two guys got out of the Jaguar and approached the passenger side. The car window rolled down, and Gene couldn't believe his eyes. *It's Tony! He's alive?!*

He followed them to where Tony lived. He also found out Tony owned the Broadway Automobile. He stalked them all day.

***

The next day, returning from the corner store with his newspaper and refreshments, Gene started gathering information on Tony through the Internet. He wanted revenge, and he wasn't going to wait a couple of years to exact that on Tony, but he had to plan it well and hit his weak spot. *If he's alive, then Charlene is also!*

He googled Charlene. Thumbnails of her beautiful pictures filled the computer screen. He started to daydream. With his eyes glued to the monitor, he reached for a can of energy drink and knocked his newspaper and keys to the floor, snapping him out of his reverie. Picking them up, he noticed that the car section of the paper had a list of want ads. One jumped out at him:

> *EYEWITNESS WANTED – CAR THEFT: Stolen car: Jaguar SX, license plate 'CARTER'. Contact 555-0908 if you have any information.*

Gene put the current issue aside and looked for the previous day's issue. He found it and checked the page where he'd written the license plate of the Jaguar he saw the day before: *CARTER*. Yes, the same car.

He put on his jacket, pocketed his keys, and left the apartment. He walked several blocks until he found a phone booth. He dropped a quarter in the slot and dialed the number on the newspaper page.

The phone rang at the house of Pete Carter, the owner of the stolen Jaguar. As Pete rushed to it, almost knocking over a potted plant in the process, his wife yelled at him, "Let's hope this call is about the car you allowed to get stolen, you idiot."

Pete, an up-and-coming insurance executive, picked up the phone, shielding one ear against the noise of his domestic chaos. "Hello?" His two kids ran past, screaming as they chased each other. Outside, the neighborhood dogs were barking.

"I'm calling about your ad in the paper regarding the stolen car," said the unknown voice.

Pete's eyes widened, and he smiled in relief. "Yes, yes, I'm listening. Do you know where it is? Who stole it?"

"No, I don't know," answered Gene, "but I'd like to help you."

The smile left Pete's face. "What? What do you mean?"

"I'm an electrical engineer, and car alarms are my specialty. I have an idea on how to catch the thieves who stole your car, and I may have a lead—"

"What lead? What are you talking about? I don't understand."

What an idiot, Gene thought to himself. Then he said into the phone, "Meet me in front of Broadway Automobile at noon, sharp. I'll explain then."

Pete started to panic. "Hey, who are you? Where are you calling from?"

"Just meet me there if you want your car back." Gene hung up the phone.

Pete left his house and grabbed a taxi. *How am I gonna be able to afford a new car?* he wondered. *I blew ALL my insurance already IN THAT COMPANY.* To distract himself, he picked up a discarded newspaper on the taxi's backseat and thumbed through it. Though he could barely concentrate on the words before him, one item in the daily police report jumped out: *Vehicle theft: Bugatti Veyron, known for its 1000 hp and top speed of 253.52 mph has been stolen from the shopping mall. The market price could reach 2 million dollars.*

Pete folded the newspaper. At least, he wasn't the only one in town to get an expensive car stolen. But there's still no word about his Jaguar.

The taxi dropped Pete off in front of Broadway Automobile. He got out carrying a fat manila envelope stuffed with the Jaguar's papers.

Gene, wearing a hooded jacket and a pair of glasses, approached. "Good afternoon."

"Is it?" asked Pete. "Are you the guy who called me?"

"Yes to both questions if you're the guy who just had his Jag stolen," said Gene, with a thin smile.

"And why should I listen to anything you have to say?" demanded Pete.

"You got a better plan?"

"Uh . . ."

"What's with the papers?"

"History of the Jag."

"Good, that'll help."

They stepped aside to allow an attractive young woman with a little white poodle on a leash to enter the dealership. The poodle snarled and barked at Pete. The woman gave him a withering stare as she and her pet crossed through the doorway and into the showroom.

"I hate dogs!" exclaimed Pete. "My neighbor's little mutt yaps at me every time I walk by."

"Don't worry, we'll take care of that, too," Gene answered smoothly. "Now, go take a look at that Mercedes over there."

"How about you?" asked Pete.

"I'll be right outside. Here's something to take care of your purchase," said Gene, handing him a backpack.

"Woah! Where did you get this?" a surprised Pete asked upon checking the bag's contents.

"Don't worry; we'll get that back," assured Gene.

"Now go and buy that car," said Gene, "and then we'll nail the bastards."

***

The silver Mercedes that Pete had just purchased nearly filled the available space in Gene's tool-cluttered garage. Pete stood to the side as Gene inspected the window glass codes. Wires hung from the wheel to the floor. Gene bent under the steering wheel and connected an alarm plug. His hand-held voltmeter measured 12V. Then he added an electrical device called a Linear Actuator Motor. The Mercedes was on the crank, and his LAM was on the wheel axle. He made contact with the red wire on the LAM and sparked it, and the LAM started to move the wheel to the left. Also installed was an advanced microchip that was similar to the one used in the *Hugo* game. Gene was fascinated by what this microchip was capable of doing.

"Is it finished?" asked Pete.

Gene got up and stretched. "Oh, yeah. Now the fun can begin." He took out a ghost plate LCD license plate cover and showed it to Pete.

"Ever seen these Hide-A-Plate License LCD screens? You can write down whatever you want on it." As Gene walked past Pete to his tool bench, Pete shrank back and then accidentally dropped all the papers he was holding.

"You're still carrying around all that paperwork?" asked Gene. He finished with the installation and started putting his tools away. "Let's go for a ride," he said to Pete.

***

The Mercedes eased onto the highway, and Gene steered it into the E-Z Pass lane. He turned to Pete. "Two ways we can do this. Hack someone's transponder ID or drive right behind a car with an E-Z Pass. Keep your head down and face hidden."

They passed through the E-Z lane, and Gene swerved into the fast lane heading to the bridge. Flooring the gas pedal, he pushed the Mercedes to 90 mph. "Damn, this car can really fly."

Pete was inspecting the lights and controls on the brightly lit Mercedes dashboard. "I like this navigation system. It's fascinating."

"You know, we could actually monitor this car with it."

"Seriously? You can do that?" asked Pete.

"We could even monitor this car with a PC. All we have to do is install a GPS tracking device."

"Is that complicated?"

"No. I'll work on it, and you'll be the first to know of my progress." Glancing in the rearview mirror, Gene spotted a black car, possibly an unmarked cop car, gaining on them. He eased off the gas pedal to slow down.

"Shit!" But then he noticed the car's foreign registration plate, so he began accelerating again.

"If they can do it, we can too."

Pete, however, was not amused. "You're driving too fast; we're going to get a speeding ticket!"

"That's exactly what I want," replied Gene. "The police control speed by GPS tracking this days. But car dealers hack into the mainframe, so they know who is rich and can pay for their speeding tickets." He grinned as he glanced over at Pete.

"You're still dragging those fucking papers around?"

Pete blushed, but Gene wouldn't let up on him. "Ever toss a wad of papers through a car window at ninety miles per hour?" And with that, he grabbed the papers from the bewildered Pete and threw them out of the window. "Ahhhh . . . now that's satisfying!"

"Man, what the hell?" cried Pete. Behind them, the papers went flying through the air as the other drivers nervously honked their horns.

"You don't need those anymore! You have to be a little crazy in this line of business."

Pete glared at him, his eyes watering from the speed of the wind coming in the open window. "I guess I'll have to become a little crazier then."

Chapter 9
The Setup

Tony's enormous house—a modern, square building made entirely of black glass and silver frames—stood in an upscale neighborhood. A few lights showing from the inside faintly lit the gathering dusk. Gene parked his car some distance from the house but still within view. He watched as Tony got out of his car and walked to the front door. Tony stopped at the door, typed something into the keypad beside the front door, and entered.

Gene watched him carefully. He pulled out his cell phone and dialed Pete's number. "Hey. We got 'em."

"Got who?"

"Them. The bastards that stole your car!"

"What do you mean 'you got them'? How did you get them?"

"Long story, man. Just come and meet me."

***

Gene and Pete sat in the Mercedes, waiting. Gene closed the window of the car and looked at the codes on the glass. "Same car."

"What did you say?" asked Pete. Silence. "Come on, who is he then?"

"Be patient, man. You'll find out," said Gene as Tony left the house, got in the M8, and drove off. "I'll go to the front door and check out his alarm system."

"Okay, I'll cover you till you hack it," said Pete.

Gene sniffed. "I don't hack, I crack." He went to the front door, looked around, and entered the hallway. He inspected the walls and ceiling for a possible surveillance system. Nothing. He noticed a complicated lock with a keypad to deactivate the alarm. He returned to the car where Pete waited.

"We're lucky. There's no video surveillance or mini-cameras, but there's a complicated alarm system on the front door."

"How do we get in then?" asked Pete.

Gene cracked a sly smile. "You mean how do we break in? First, we sniff around a little bit. If we want to find out what kind of code he's typing in, we'll just install a mini-cam."

Just then Pete's phone rang, and he broke off to answer it. "This is Jack Masters," said the tense voice. "I've been calling you all week about my insurance payment."

Pete grimaced. "I'll get back to you. I'm very busy at the moment." He hung up.

Pete's phone rang. "Who is it now?"

"Where the hell are you!?" came an angry female voice. Pete's wife.

He hung up without speaking to her. "I'm a reckless guy now!" Pete declared.

***

The following evening, Gene and Pete arrived in a mobster-looking van. Gene stepped out of the van dressed like a cable guy. He carried a step ladder and a tool bag. He looked around and saw no one. He approached the house and entered the hallway.

"Welcome." The melodious female voice came from the alarm system speaker.

Gene froze and looked around again. He noticed the sensor above the door with wires leading to the speaker. He smiled in relief and with renewed confidence. Picking out a spot with a good view of the keypad, he set up the mini-cam.

Later that night, Gene and Pete watched Tony's house from inside the van. Pete was still worried. "Won't he see it?"

"No," said Gene. "I found the perfect place for it." He opened his laptop and pulled up a search engine tab, then typed in *Axis video server*.

The screen display showed:

http://152.1.130.216/view/index.shtml
http://152.1.130.217/view/index.shtml
http://152.1.130.218/view/index.shtml

"Now you see how to crack into remote private CCTV cameras," he explained to Pete.

Gene clicked on one of the links. The screen displayed view from the camera over the pool. He clicked the second link, and up came a view of cramped, cluttered office. The two people in the scene were busy having sex.

"C'mon, man. Give them some privacy," said Pete.

Gene typed: *intitle: 'live view TONY#1/-AXIS'*, and the camera image showed the front door and the keyboard for entry codes. "That's it!"

***

Tony returned. He pulled into the driveway, got out of the car, and walked up the front steps. From inside the van, Gene and Pete watched the monitor closely as he typed in the pass code on the keypad.

"And that's how you get a private code," said Gene. "Now, all we have to do is wait   for him to leave again. I hope he doesn't do anything crazy in the next few hours."

Once again, the van carrying Gene and Pete arrived the next evening in front of the house just as Tony drove away in the M8. Getting out of the van, Gene took two silver suitcases out of the van and gave one to Pete.

"Is that all?" asked Pete.

"Yeah, let's go."

They got to the main entrance. *"Welcome,"* sounded the alarm's dulcet voice.

"Interesting," said Pete, as they both smiled.

Gene typed in the entrance code. Click. The door opened on a huge foyer decorated with fine art and marble floors.

"Nice place he lives in," observed Pete.

"You would, too, if you could afford it," stated Gene.

They crossed the foyer to the living room. Pete took a step, but Gene pulled him back. "Stop!"

"Why?"

"Something's wrong. There's gotta be something more in here." He took out his cell phone.

"IR diodes. If you don't see any red coming out, try using your cell phone camera to view the output. IR shows up as white on cameras and is invisible to human eyes. Look how many infrared rays there are." He showed the display to Pete.

"What are we going to do now?"

Gene took an infrared pointer out of his pocket and turned it on. He directed the pointer first to the left then to the right. "Which is the source, and which is the receiving side? We'll bluff, and see what happens."

He directed the infrared ray onto the left side, exactly in the center of the receptor in the wall. Gene redirected the light with his light. And with his free right hand, he closed the original light spot. Nothing happened.

"Got it." He smiled to himself and turned off the light. "Tricks of the trade," he said to Pete. "Even the Pink Panther doesn't know about this stuff."

Pete looked at him quizzically. "What are we going to do now?"

"I'll turn off this part of the alarm. It'll be like it never existed. We're in now."

Gene took out his chewing gum and stuck it to the pointer. Then he stuck the pointer to the receptor. Once they got inside and found the main box, Gene reprogrammed the alarm. All of the infrared lights were now shut down.

"Phew, I feel better now," said Pete.

Gene scanned the ceiling. "Here, I found a place for the mini-cam," he said to Pete. "It's easy. See the spot behind that light?"

"Yeah."

"Here's a screwdriver. All you need to do is screw it into the ceiling."

Pete started putting the camera into place, but he dropped the screwdriver.

"Yeah, smash it to pieces," said Gene.

"I only dropped the screwdriver."

"Don't worry, man. I've dropped it a hundred times myself."

They left the living room and came to the entrance gate through a hall. They opened the gate and carefully shut it behind them.

Back in the van, Gene turned on the monitors, bringing up the displays from inside the entrance gate, hall, living room, and the kitchen. "All set. Big Brother is officially watching."

Then they waited. Gene had fallen asleep sitting up, and Pete was growing tired. He nudged Gene. "We have to arrange night shifts. Nothing happens during the day here."

"I'm going to go get me some food." Gene yawned.

"Just don't buy candy."

"I only buy candy when we have girls working on the case," Gene laughed. "You want something?"

"No, I'm good."

When Gene returned to the van, he carried a sack of take-out burgers. "I bought you something. I don't want to eat alone."

"Okay." Pete took the burger and began to devour it. Ketchup dripped down his shirt. "Damn, this is messy! What do they put in these things?"

"So, you're not as sophisticated as you used to be?" Gene said as he munched his burger.

Pete smiled. "Hey, you shouldn't talk with your mouth full! Didn't you learn that in school?"

"I prefer practice over theory."

Pete scratched his left eye and plucked out a couple of eyelashes. He inspected them in his palm. "Luck!" he whispered to himself.

The hallway monitor flickered, drawing their attention to it. On the screen, they saw Tony arrive with a beautiful blond woman, Charlene.

"Charlene . . . " Gene whispered to himself.

***

As Gene and Pete watched from inside the van, Tony and Charlene walked through the hall and came to the living room. They each took an armchair to sit in, but Tony immediately got up and went to the bar. He poured a whiskey on the rocks, then slowly returned to Charlene and handed her the drink. As she sipped, he started touching her on the shoulder and then all over.

She flinched away. "Don't . . . Not tonight, Tony . . . I'm not in the mood. I'm tired. Tomorrow, okay?"

He got up and returned to the mini-bar.

Charlene continued to voice her thoughts. "What are we going to do about the debts at the casino?"

Tony stepped along the wall and took down a small painting, revealing a safe. He opened the safe and took out a bank book.

"Twenty million dollars in the bank, baby, and it's all cash," he said, showing her the bank book. "See? All I have to do is go and pick it up. I could cover Marco Milione's body with banknotes."

Charlene gave him a brilliant smile.

In the van, Gene and Pete watched and listened to the monitor's playback. At the sound of "twenty million" in Tony's voice, Gene was filled with rage: *And half of that is mine!*

"Twenty million dollars!" exclaimed Pete. "We're gonna fuck his world over. And you won't have to worry about cash for a long time."

In the living room, Tony paced back and forth. He approached Charlene, then drew away. "Well, okay, if you're not in the mood."

"I trust you," she said. "Have I ever doubted you? It's just that . . . you know I'm paying back your debts to Marco."

He finished his drink. She quickly checked her makeup in a small mirror she took from her handbag. Then they got up and left the house. In silence, they got into the car and drove off. They didn't notice that Gene and Pete were following them.

Casino Street was all bright lights and crowds of people. Tony dropped Charlene off in front of the casino, kissed her, and drove away. Alone in the car, he shook his head. *I've been with her too long. This isn't working anymore,* he thought.

***

Gene drove the van slowly along Casino Street as he made plans with Pete. "You'll have to dress up a little bit. Get a tux, come to this casino, and meet up with her. The blond woman. Name's Charlene."

"Not a problem," Pete smiled.

An hour later, Pete arrived at the casino, dressed in a tuxedo. He walked across the red-and-black carpeted floor to the roulette table. Working in her hostess capacity, Charlene noticed him right away.

"Evening, handsome," she purred.

"Good evening to you, too, pretty thing. How are you?" Pete called up all his charm and laid it on thick.

"Better now, and you?"

"Mmm! Not bad, I feel lucky." He spotted a player giving up and leaving. "This seat isn't taken anymore, is it? Mind if I throw some dice?"

"Why not?" smiled Charlene. She announced to the croupier, "Incoming player." She nodded to Pete as a signal to introduce himself.

"Name's Jack."

"Like jackpot," Charlene giggled.

"Exactly." He tossed some dice, doing his best to look like the smooth and suave rich guy he wanted to show her. Then, to his relief, he won a couple of rounds.

"Think I've had enough for tonight," he said to Charlene. "Let's have a drink. What do you say?"

"Sure, after I finish here," she replied. "Sit over there and I'll be along in a minute."

Pete sat at the bar and ordered a drink. He watched Charlene as she walked through the casino, attracting the attention of every customer on her way.

Finally, she returned to Pete. "Been waiting long?"

"Just enjoying watching you, sweetheart," he said. "So where's the real game? A friend of a friend told me I could find some high stakes here."

"Oh, you know about the game?" she said. "Follow me, and I'll show you where they're playing."

Charlene led him up to the main poker room, in which six or seven tuxedoed men sat around the game table. The air was thick with cigarette and cigar smoke.

"Here's a new player," Charlene said as she introduced Pete to the group. "His name is Jack, like jackpot."

Tony nodded. "Okay, Jack, I like your style. I wish you were a policeman, too. You'd be very useful to us."

"Policeman my ass. I'm a detective."

"Funny man." Tony tapped the desk with his hand and lit a cigar.

"Just kidding," joked Pete. "I'm an executive. I work for an insurance company."

"We can use those kinds of people, too," said Tony.

"Basically, I overcharge by a few percent on an insurance contract and keep that extra percentage. For sure, I could get a better payoff on car insurance for you."

"Yeah, go for it," Tony said approvingly. "He who knows the job, knows the tricks of the trade. Let's play."

They played for some time. Tony picked up a bottle of whiskey in his hand and looked at the label.

"Do you like bottles with forty-four percent printed on them?" he asked. Then he slapped Charlene on her bottom.

She pushed him away. "You've been drinking again."

"Shut up and let me play," snarled Tony.

Pete coughed a little and nodded to Tony. "Yeah, but fifty-five percent sounds better."

"He's quick!" smiled Tony as he threw in his cards. So much for that hand.

The game drew to a close. Tony stood up and looked around the table. "Okay, then. We'll see each other next Thursday."

A voice came from the far side of the table. "I can't. I really can't. My daughter is getting married."

"And what will she get from a cheap bastard like you?" said Tony, to the laughter of the group.

Pete asked, "So then we've got a meeting next Thursday?" Everyone nodded. "Sounds good to me."

***

Pete returned to the van in the parking lot, where Gene sat waiting for him. "Next Thursday, they're playing a big game," said Pete. "Tony will probably draw some money from his bank account earlier that day."

"So we've got to organize something for next week, then."

"What do you mean? Take his money?" asked Pete.

"They're Mafia guys; it's too risky to expose ourselves." Gene paused a bit, thinking. Then he said, "Listen. You could play another role."

"Again?"

Gene raised his eyebrows and smiled. "Take a look in the rear-view mirror and say hello to Mr. Tony."

"No way!"

"We've come this far. We might as well go all the way. You go to the bank and collect the money instead of him."

"That idea is terrible! Isn't there some easier way to get twenty million?"

Gene was adamant. "He's probably only got small change in the safe. For that kind of money, is this shit worth it? We've got to take more. All of it! Twenty million!"

"You make it sound so easy. How will we do it without getting caught?"

"Leave that to me," said Gene. "First, we'll wait and see when and how much he'll take out of the bank."

"You're serious about this, aren't you?" Pete asked, incredulous.

***

Tony arrived home the following afternoon. He walked into the living room and poured himself a drink. Then he opened the safe and took out the bank book. He dialed the number of the bank on his cordless phone.

Inside the van, Gene and Pete were watching him through the camera. "This is it," said Gene. "He's making the call to the bank. You just keep going; you'll see what happens later."

61

They watched as Tony sat in one of the chairs, drink in one hand and phone held to his ear with the other. Gene adjusted the pick-up on their listening mike to make sure they could hear what he was saying:

"Hello. I have an account with you, and I'd like to withdraw four hundred thousand dollars next Thursday." Tony's voiced dripped with confidence. *"Yes. The account number is . . . ."*

Gene and Pete listened intently. Gene counted on his well-developed memory to retain the account number, while Pete scribbled it on a scrap of paper.

"Next Thursday, four hundred thousand dollars. Right. Yes, I will pick it up before noon." Tony put the phone down and took another sip of his drink.

"This is the plan," said Gene to his fellow conspirator. "You're gonna call the bank and order this two with seven zeros."

"What? That's everything he's got."

"He's got twenty million dollars and some change, which we'll leave him."

"Yeah, leave him a couple cents," agreed Pete. "And how will we take out the money?"

"You're gonna call the bank. We've got the account number. And if you have to, you'll go to the bank."

"What?" questioned Pete. "Who the hell do you think I am? A delivery boy? I don't even look like him."

"So? Doesn't matter . . . Nobody knows you. We are living in an electronic age. Who the fuck cares about your face? If you wish, we could call him to check if he knows the director of the bank."

"How are you going to do that? Don't be stupid."

"Listen, this kind of bank account is for off-shore use," said Gene. He dialed the number; a tiny recorded voice echoed out his phone's speaker. "Stupid voice mail."

"Hey, I'm not going to talk to him," Pete protested.

Gene pressed number five on the keypad. The tinny voice instructed, *"Please enter the three-digit password."* Gene typed in 777, the standard default for most password systems. The first message was replayed: *"Tony, you can come tonight and fuck me like crazy."* Charlene's voice.

"Okay," Gene said to Pete after they'd replayed the message and stopped laughing. "Here's the plan. You'll be dressed like him. You'll shave and that's that. No big deal."

"He's got a mole on his left cheek," Pete commented.

"Good thinking. You'll have to work on that, man. That's your part of the job anyway. Mine is typing. Listen, man, we are getting that twenty million in cash."

Pete left the van, but quickly returned. "Hey, you didn't give me the bank's phone number."

Gene started to write the number on a piece of paper. "Wait! You can't phone the bank using his telephone."

"Why not?"

"There's a phone booth just around the corner. We have to be careful."

"You think his phone is being tapped?" asked Pete.

Gene shrugged. "It's for our own safety. The fewer clues, the better."

"It's your show."

"And I don't know the bank's phone number." Gene opened his cell phone and changed the SIM card.

"Now what are you doing?" asked Pete.

"Changing my SIM card."

"What for?"

"This number's not registered in my name."

"But they can trace our call, can't they?"

"Cell phones don't work like normal phones. They communicate through the cell towers."

"So, they're tracing us right now?"

"No way, man. We just have to drive to the other side of the town and keep moving so they can't pick us up." At Pete's look of alarm, Gene shook his head and laughed. "I'm just kidding, man. Who is going to trace a 411 call anyways?"

Pete sighed and left. Gene crumpled the unused paper and tossed it out the window.

As Pete walked up to the door of Tony's house, the alarm chimed and said *"Hello."*

Pete gasped, exclaiming, "That alarm gets me every time." He stood in the hallway, typing the code. The doors opened, and he climbed up the steps. As soon as he got in the living room, he noticed that the infrared rays had been turned off. He removed the painting from the wall and took the paper with the code: 20087000.

"Damn, what shitty handwriting. Who can read this?"

He typed in the code, and the safe door suddenly popped open with a click. "Fuck these automatic things." Then he quickly removed the bank book, sneaking a look at the figures out of curiosity.

"Fuck! That's a lot of money." He tucked the bank book in his pocket and returned to the van.

"Got everything," he reported to Gene. "Man, you've got some shitty handwriting."

"So how much does he have in the account?" asked Gene.

"You won't believe it! Twenty million eighty-seven thousand dollars!"

"Well, we'll leave him the eighty-seven thousand dollars since he counts it so carefully every day. He's going to need it badly."

They got in the van and drove to a phone booth. Pete dropped a quarter in the coin slot to dial 411 and get the bank's phone number. Then he made the call.

"Hello," said Pete in his smooth voice. "I spoke to a woman earlier. I'm Tony Donatelli, and I requested four hundred thousand dollars for next Monday, no sorry, Thursday."

"I need to check that. Wait a minute, please," said the bank clerk. "Yes, you're right. Four hundred thousand dollars for next Thursday."

"If it's possible, I'd like to change the amount. I need more cash," said Pete, stuttering for a moment. "Twenty million dollars, to be exact . . . If it's possible."

"Sir, that's a rather large amount of money. You'll have to come to the bank personally and talk with my supervisor."

"I see. When can I come?"

"You can come tomorrow before eleven a.m. That's when we deal with money orders."

"Sounds good. See you then."

"Thank you for choosing Golden Bank. We are always at your service."

Pete was gasping for breath as he hurried back to the van. "We have a problem!"

"Now what?"

"I have to go to the bank personally to arrange things."

Gene thought for a moment. "We don't have a choice. Get dressed and go. This is the best time to do it. We have everything. It's now or never."

Pete got in and leaned into the van's side door, knocking his head against the window glass. "Ow," he said, rubbing his head. "Remind me never to play poker again! Nothing but trouble comes out of gambling."

***

The next morning, Gene stopped the van in front of Pete's house and dropped him off. Pete entered and found the normal household chaos going on.

His little daughter ran by, calling out, "Hi, Daddy!" He kissed her on the cheek and took a cracker from a bowl on the dining table. Then he walked to his bedroom and took a suit from the closet, throwing it on the bed. Watching his reflection in the mirror, he dressed and fixed his tie. "Not bad," he said with satisfaction.

Quickly going to his wife's bedroom, he found an eyebrow pencil and painted a little mole on his left cheek. He vaguely heard his wife yelling about something from somewhere in the house. He walked through the hallway back to the front door, passing his daughter who gave him a puzzled look.

Pete walked out of his house and immediately cringed at the barking of his neighbor's annoying yappy dog. He heard Gene call from the van, "Check this out, man!"

Gene pushed a button on a small remote, and a very high frequency signal made the dog squeal and run away. Grinning, Pete climbed in the van and shut the door. "Hey, thanks," he said, looking at the remote that Gene held.

Gene shrugged. "I had that same problem once."

They arrived at the bank. Pete got out of the van and said to Gene, "Keep your fingers crossed. If anything goes wrong, we'll be finished."

"Hey, you're an employee in one of the best insurance companies in the world. You look good. You're a business type!"

"You're right," Pete agreed. "I look damn good." He walked up to the bank, stopping near the door to check his appearance reflected in the glass.

Chapter 10

Bank Heist

"Everything's taken care of," Pete said as they drove along in the van.

"Yeah?" asked Gene. "What are we gonna do about Tony?"

"If you think we should shoot him, forget it. That's going too far," Pete replied, shaking his head.

"That would be the Mafia way." Gene shifted the van's gears and sighed. His voice sounded tired as he went on, "Look, we don't have much time. We have to get him out of the way. I think you should throw a little party at your house on Wednesday."

"What for?" exclaimed Pete. "Isn't the heist next Thursday?"

"Right, we have to pick up the money on Thursday," answered Gene. "If he picks up that money before we do, we're totally screwed. So, we need to act before then. You should throw a party the day before, where we can distract him, so he can't pick up the money on Thursday."

Pete rolled his eyes. "What kind of a mess have I gotten myself into?"

"What about me?"

"You think it's easy to organize a party in two days?"

"Look," said Gene, "invite Tony and his girl over to your place. In the meantime, we'll hire a hooker. He adores blondes, so we'll get a blond hooker. Make sure it's a real blond, no dark roots or anything. He's Sicilian, and Sicilian dudes just prefer blondes, but they're absolutely obsessed with having the real thing. A local 'bottle blonde' is just kind of a mediocre consolation prize in place of the real deal."

He went on, "You can tell the hooker to seduce him or even drug him. Whatever, anything goes. And he'll wake up in the middle of nowhere the day after. In the meantime, we will do our job."

"It'll be tricky to do all that in one night," said Pete. Then he brightened with a new thought. "But . . . I'll get the chance to get back at him for stealing my car."

"You should be thanking me for this," Gene grinned as he handed Pete a piece of paper. "Here's his number."

"Okay, okay. I'm grateful. Except, we can't do this at my house. And where do we find a blond hooker?"

"You're right. We'll use a borrowed place. I have a buddy who's got a nice condo, and he owes me a favor. As for the hooker," Gene laughed, "that's the easiest part. Go to Casino Street, and you'll find plenty of them!"

"So when do we start?"

"Tonight. I'll arrange for the condo, and you go find your blond hooker."

Pete snorted, "MY blond hooker? Don't get any ideas." He shook his head, grinning.

***

Pete drove the Mercedes through the downtown streets. Night was falling as the car's GPS navigator announced his trajectory: *"Your current location is . . . Casino Street."* Lots of tuned sports cars were cruising the street as Pete drove around. He noticed the ladies of the night gathering beneath the streetlamps. Time to start looking for a blond one.

But first, he had a call to make. He dialed Tony's number, and when it was picked up, he said into his cell phone, "Hey, Tony, how's it going?"

"Who's this?" Tony's voice showed surprise.

Pete mentally crossed his fingers and took a deep breath. "Hey, it's Jack. Jackpot. From the poker game. We played together the other night."

"Sorry, man," answered Tony. *"I didn't recognize your voice. What's up?"*

"How about coming over to my place on Wednesday?"

"Wednesday?" Tony paused for a moment. *"I think I can make it. If Charlene is okay with that."*

"Oh, I didn't know you were in a relationship," Pete said in his most apologetic tone. "Sorry, man. I flirted with her a little . . ."

"No problem. Go for it. Who's gonna be at your place besides you and me?"

"Well, I got problems with the wife. You know how it goes. Time for a change . . . Got her to take a weekend away . . . you know, for her." Pete broke off abruptly as his attention was caught by the red light ahead. Slamming on the brakes just in time to avoid running the light, he also noticed an interesting figure standing on the curb.

"You still there?" asked Tony. *"Why'd you stop talking?"*

"I'm driving in my car, so I'm not fully concentrating. And . . . I just saw a hot blond chick a couple of seconds ago."

The item that had drawn Pete's attention was a beautiful blond hooker walking by. Her red leather mini-skirt showed off her long legs as she strode confidently in her high heels. Pete waved through the open and called her to join him.

On the phone, Tony voiced his agreement. *"So, pick her up."*

"Don't worry I've got it under control," Pete told him. "And, as I was saying, I'm involved with someone and was thinking we could get together sometime . . . The four of us." As Pete spoke, his eyes remained fixed on the hooker approaching his car.

"You suggesting a swap or a four-way?" Tony asked.

Pete laughed, "Whatever you want."

"Okay. Fine with me. Excellent," said Tony. *"Change is always good, but I warn you, that Charlene is a dangerous chick."*

Aware that the blond woman was almost at his door, Pete rushed the conversation to a close. "Then, it's Wednesday at ten thirty. That work for you?"

"Sounds great," replied Tony as he rang off.

The blonde leaned into Pete's window. She had a big smile on her face as she asked, "You want something?"

Turning off the radio, Pete looked at her and said, "Yeah, you, only you."

"Can I come in?" She didn't wait for him to answer as she opened the door and sat in the passenger seat.

"You surprised me," Pete said appreciatively. "A point for you."

"So what are you waiting for?" she asked, winking at him. "You're my kind of guy."

"Oh, am I? The real deal . . ." He turned the radio back on and pumped up the volume.

"Ah, music. Are we gonna have a long chat?" She settled back in her seat.

"I'm a lucky guy. I bumped into a real hot blond chick."

"I don't usually work the streets. This is a rich neighborhood, so here I am . . ."

"What's your name, sugar?"

"My name is Mysterious," she smiled. "But my friends call me Mysti."

"Seriously? Mysterious? Another point for you. You're going to beat me in this game."

"I think you're the romantic type." She leaned a little closer to him.

Pete sighed, "I was . . . until a couple days ago."

"Why, what happened? Women are tough, huh?"

Pete smiled. "Mysti, do you know how to seduce a guy? You know, down to the bones?"

"I guess I was wrong about you," she said, shaking her head. "You're not as romantic as you look. Well, yes, it depends."

"For five hundred dollars."

"Five hundred?" she scoffed. "Can't you do better than that?"

"Okay," Pete sighed, "I can go to one thousand, but—"

Mysti smiled. "Honey, for a grand I can do anything."

***

"I think this is the place," said Tony. He and Charlene were driving through a neighborhood filled with deluxe apartments and condos. Flowers spilled over the apartment balconies and fountains played in the courtyards.

Charlene noticed a flower shop on the corner. "Don't you think we should get something for them?" She got out of the car and went into the flower shop.

Flowers in hand, they climbed the external spiral-shaped stairs to their destination. Mysti had already seen them from the window. She opened the door, all smiles. "Ooh, there you are. Finally. How are you tonight?"

"We almost didn't find you," Charlene said, handing her the flowers. "I didn't even know that this part of town existed." She caught Tony noticing the woman's breasts bulging above the low-cut cleavage of her red dress.

Tony pushed forward into the room, carrying the bottle of whiskey he'd brought as his offering. He headed to the bar in the corner of the living room, opened the bottle, and poured a drink.

Mysti continued her conversation with Charlene. "Jack is very romantic. He wants to live away from the city life. You know what I mean? Peaceful neighborhood."

"That's totally how he is," Charlene nodded. "I got to know him a little." She walked around the apartment, looking appreciatively at the tasteful furnishings. "It's such a beautiful place. Where's Jack?"

"In the bathroom. He'll be out in a minute." Mysti looked over at Tony, who had gulped his whiskey and was trying to suppress a cough.

Tony looked up as Pete came out of the bathroom, his hair still wet from the shower. "Here's the man," Tony exclaimed. "My friend, where the hell you been? You left me with these two beauties to handle." Mysti smiled knowingly, while Charlene looked coldly at him.

"You mean you didn't take advantage of the situation?" said Pete. "Ha!" He dried his hair with a towel. "Should have gone for it while you had the chance." He glanced at Charlene, who mumbled something and looked away. She was visibly ticked off.

"Women! Can't live with them, can't live without them," said Tony. He smiled at Charlene. "I'm a fair player, aren't I, baby?" She ignored him but remained calm.

Tony walked over to Pete and handed him a drink. "I'll have to show you what I do for a living."

Surprised, Pete almost spilled his drink. "The car business, you mean?" he asked.

"Right." Tony coughed.

Pete shook his head. "I don't know shit about cars. Mercedes makes cars for women."

"Don't bullshit me. You drive a Mercedes with Brabus decor."

"I bought that from Broadway Automobile," said Pete.

Tony's attention was divided. He was staring at Mysti. She blew him a kiss and smiled.

"Aaah, everyone's so friendly here! Who wants another drink?" Tony said, putting on a show of hosting from the bar.

Charlene glared at him fiercely and walked out to the balcony. It was decorated as tastefully as the apartment, and displayed an aquarium with lights inside. Charlene studied the aquarium, which had a small turtle colony inside. She touched the glass. *I know how you feel, little turtles,* she thought. She realized it was her life as Tony's girl that was trapping her, making her feel like a small turtle behind glass. *How did that happen?* she wondered as she went back to the group in the living room.

"It's so nice here," Charlene said brightly. "I really like this place. I'd like to live in an apartment like this."

Tony shrugged. "Too small for me. I like bigger places."

Mysti chimed in, "It is tiny, but some people like it that way. I find it rather cozy myself." She sat on the couch and winked at Tony. She liked playing the perfect hostess. This gig sure beat the usual tricks she turned with her sleazy, but well-heeled clients.

"It's small, but it's a good investment. Jack knew what he was doing when he bought this place." Tony approached Mysti and offered her a drink.

"Thanks," said Mysti. "I'm so thirsty."

Charlene had had enough. She stomped out of the apartment, brushing against Pete as she left. The door slammed behind her.

"What just happened?" inquired a puzzled Pete.

"Go after her," Tony said, nudging him.

Pete nodded to Tony while thinking about how much he was going to enjoy wiping the smile off Tony's face. On his way out the door,

Pete winked at Mysti, and she winked back. Tony, pouring another drink at the bar, didn't notice them.

Mysti got up from the couch and sidled over to Tony. "They're so lame, the two of them. They really don't know how to live." She traced her fingers lightly down his arm.

"You're so right," he said. He turned to her and swept his hand down her side and along her legs till he reached the hem of her short skirt. When his hand started to move upward, it was beneath her skirt, on the inside of her thigh.

Mysti squirmed seductively. "Mmmm, you're a tough guy. I can see that. And you'd like it a bit rougher, wouldn't you?"

He took one more long sip from the glass and coughed. "Yeah, I like it rough."

"Feels good . . . Keep going," she sighed as she leaned closer to him

Now, he had his arm around her, holding her close. "Can I call you Wild Thing?" he breathed into her hair.

"Oooh, baby, you can call me anything you want," she purred. Then she pulled back and looked at him. "Let's go back to my place, shall we? It's a little more . . . private."

***

Outside in the apartment's courtyard, Pete found Charlene sitting alone on a concrete bench. He sat down beside her. "Why did you leave?" he asked softly.

"I don't know," she answered, her voice quivering as she held back her tears. Then she went quiet.

"Come on, nothing happened," Pete said in a jocular tone, trying to cheer her up. She still didn't speak, so he took out his cell phone. "Excuse me; I've got to make a call."

Charlene whipped around to face him, her expression showing her anger. "Who the fuck are you gonna call at this hour? Screw you," she said as she stood up and walked out of the courtyard.

"Hey, wait a minute. Stop!" Pete called, but she had vanished into the shadows of the dark street. He sighed to himself, *You weren't my priority tonight anyway, baby.*

***

Gene was chatting with a girl on the Internet when his phone rang. He'd almost gotten her to agree to go with him on a Caribbean cruise, when the phone's shrilling got on his nerves. Seeing that it was Pete calling, he forgot completely about the girl. He powered down his computer and answered his phone. "Hey, what's up? How'd it go?"

"Took you long enough to answer," complained Pete. "What are you doing right now?"

"Chatting with a girl online."

"So that's where you're spending our money! Don't spend all of it. He totally gave in to that hooker."

"Oh yeah?" said Gene. He smiled. "That's what I like to hear."

"In fact . . ." Pete drawled. He had just seen Tony and Mysti leaving by the back door of the apartment. "This is great," Pete continued. "She lured him to her place."

***

Tony and Mysti entered the motel room and closed the door. Leaning against the door, he began to touch and kiss her.

"Wait!" said Mysti. "Give me a minute to freshen up." She took the bottle from his hands and pushed him away from her.

"Hurry up," he said. "I'm yearning for you."

"So get comfortable on the bed and wait for me," she replied as she disappeared into the bathroom. There she took a bottle of sleeping pills from her purse. She poured some whiskey into a glass and crushed a few of the sleeping pills, which she added to the glass. Carrying the spiked drink, she carefully opened the bathroom door and went to the bed, now occupied by a naked Tony.

"Well, don't you look comfortable," she said, smiling. She knelt like a tiger beside the bed and kissed him. Then she held the glass to his mouth, so he could take a long sip.

"Ahhh," sighed Tony. "That's exactly what I need." A satisfied smile spread across his face.

She took the glass from his mouth and kissed him passionately. The drink spilled all over the blanket. Taking his head in her hands, she pulled him towards her and pressed his body to hers. Her nails scratched eagerly over his skin.

***

Pete awoke early the next morning. Unable to sleep, he looked at the clock, got up, and made some coffee. He sipped it as he dialed Mysti's phone number.

She answered in a tired voice, "Ooooh, what now? It's so early . . ."

"Is it done?" Pete snapped.

Recognizing his voice, Mysti rolled over in her silk sheets. "Yeah, when I left the motel, he was sleeping like a baby." She stretched luxuriously.

"Good job." He hung up, ready to get to work on the rest of the plan.

"Well, good night then," drawled Mysti, unaware the connection had been cut off. "Ooops." She went to hang up the phone but missed the phone base. The handset fell to the floor. She was asleep before it landed.

***

Pete arrived at Tony's house. As he walked up to the front door, a well-modulated *"Hello"* came from the alarm system's speakers.

Pete glared up at the speakers. "I'm really sick of hearing your voice," he snarled. As if the mechanical monitor could answer him.

After ringing the doorbell and making sure no one was home, Pete typed the entrance code into the front door's keypad. The door opened. He walked in and went straight to the picture that hid the safe in the living room. He took down the painting and opened the safe. He removed the bank book, closed the safe, and put back the painting. Then he left the house and got back in the Mercedes. He checked his watch.

Dressed in his "Tony" persona, complete with fake mole on his left cheek, Pete walked up to the private teller at Golden Bank's main office. "My name is Tony Donatelli," he introduced himself, taking the bank book out of his pocket. "I've got an appointment."

The clerk asked him to take a seat as she went to locate the manager. When the manager arrived, Pete stood up and shook his hand.

"We've been expecting you, Mr. Donatelli," said the manager. "Please come this way."

Pete followed him to the secured vault at the back of the bank. Rows of gray metal shelves were heavily protected behind a steel grate. The security guard opened the door with a key hanging from a metal chain, then he stepped back to watch as the manager removed the cash bags one by one. He carefully put them on the desk, saying to Pete, "You may count it all. It's yours."

Pete picked one pile of crisp notes and flicked through them. "I'm done," he said.

Pete left the bank carrying cash bags in the trunk of his Mercedes. Barely able to contain his excitement, he got in the car, shut the door, and pumped his fist. *Yeah!* He pumped his fist again for good measure. Then he took out his cell phone and called Gene.

***

Gene was standing in the kitchen with an egg in his hands. The phone rang. Smash! The egg landed on the floor as Gene grabbed the phone. "Damn! What comes around, goes around," he cursed as he pressed the answer button. "Hello?"

Pete was on the line, "Hey. What's up with you, buddy? I'm driving through the city. I'm about to take the highway to your place, ninety miles per hours, baby. The papers you threw away when we were driving on the highway will lead me to you." He laughed.

"You got the money?" Gene interrupted.

"Yeah, yeah!" crowed Pete. "Woo-hoo! Full throttle, man!"

"Well, drive safely," Gene answered. "I want you to get here with all of it! Sweet revenge!" He looked at his computer monitor before hanging up. The display showed the coordinates and map of Pete's location; the red dot moved rapidly along the route he'd described.

When Pete got to Gene's place, he hit the brakes hard as he parked the Mercedes in front of the building. Running up the stairs as fast as he could go, Pete walked in on Gene who was hunched over his computer, playing the *Hugo* game. Pete entered the room and dropped some cash bags onto Gene's desk.

"What kind of kid's game are you playing?" Pete asked, glancing at the display on the computer screen. "Help me unload the bags!"

"Everybody has some kind of hang-up from their childhood. Any advanced use of the microchip in this game is far beyond a little child's toy, " Gene answered as he went outside to get more cash bags.

Pete opened one of the bags. "Take a look. Plenty of green at last."

"I told you cash is king. So now you can do whatever you wanna do," said Gene.

"Enjoy it while you can and remember to insure yourself, so you don't end up like Tony."

"I will."

"Insurance is what we're going to need, man," said Gene.

Gene settled back in his chair and re-started the computer game as the door closed behind Pete.

Chapter 11
Genius Revenge

A lone in the motel room, Tony woke up with bloodshot eyes. At first, he didn't know where he was. Aside from being a mess, the room he was in had all the blandness of a generic rental accommodation. He glanced at the watch. It was almost noon. The bank—had he missed his appointment? He frantically looked around, ripping the sheets from the bed, as he searched for his cell phone. "It's gone," he said out loud as the full impact of his situation dawned on him.

"Fuck, I'm hungover." He stumbled into the bathroom and looked at himself in the mirror. There were scratches all over his body.

"Where the hell am I? Out of town? In the middle of nowhere? Look at me, what a mess!" he yelled, his mouth opening wide in a gargoyle expression of rage.

Finally, he found his car keys. He dressed quickly and went out to the parking lot. At least his car was still there. He got in and nervously inserted the key into the ignition. Still tired and hungover, he slumped forward in a near-sleep. When his head hit the car horn, he jerked upward at the sound. "Aaaaaah!" he cried. Then he pulled himself together enough to start the car and drive away towards his home.

Home at last. Tony got out of the car and ran forward, leaving the car door wide open. At the front door, he typed in the entrance code he remembered.

"Wrong code. Try again, please." The alarm system's carefully modulated voice was maddening.

"What the fuck? Isn't that the code?" He hit the lock's keypad hard, then typed in the code once again. The door opened. He climbed up the stairs gasping for air.

In the living room, Tony took down the painting from the wall. He opened the safe and took out the bank book. He grabbed up the house phone, but the line was dead. He angrily smashed it to the floor. He went back to his car, got in, and drove away.

Twenty minutes later, Tony skipped the regular line at Golden Bank and went directly to the private teller. "Hi, my name is Tony Donatelli. I have an order in for today."

The clerk checked his records on the computer screen. "I'm sorry, Mr. Donatelli, but it seems someone has already completed this transaction. It shows a balance of eighty-seven thousand dollars in the account. The twenty-million withdrawal was made earlier today."

Tony paused, his face rapidly losing its color. He drew back his hand as if to slap the clerk. "Would you like to try again?" he demanded.

By this time, the bank's guards had been alerted and were making their way towards Tony. Looking around at the muscle heading towards him, Tony put his hands up to indicate mock surrender and walked back to the door. There, he turned and said to the bank, its clerks, the guards, the customers, and the universe as a whole, *"Destiny vi aspetterà."* Destiny waits, indeed.

Tony returned to his chop shop and secluded himself in the office. He searched through his papers. He tried to make a call, but he realized he had lost his records, along with his cell phone. *What a fucking fool I am,* he thought, *letting myself get taken in by that hooker.*

He tried dialing Charlene's number from memory, only to get a pet shop across town. He tried again. After relying so much on his cell phone, he couldn't remember her number. Everything was in the lost phone.

"Where the hell's my cell phone," he yelled at his secretary when she stuck her head in the office to see what her boss needed. The secretary shook her head and scampered back to her desk, away from his wrath.

Tony continued searching through papers on his desk, shoving file folders and catalogs onto the floor, creating a general mess. *Someone is going to pay for this,* he vowed. He picked up his car keys and left the office.

Tony pulled up in front of Charlene's house. Seeing him from her front window, she came out onto the porch. He ran up the path to the front door, but she blocked his way. She was furious. "How could you do it?" she yelled at him. "With that hooker! You creep! Fuck you, asshole." She turned and stormed back into her house.

She tried to close the front door, but Tony caught it and followed her inside. Charlene whirled around and punched Tony directly in the face. He held his chin and tried to wipe the blood from his lips. "You dumb bitch," he snarled at her, "the two of them robbed me."

"Tough cookies," Charlene snorted. "Ah, screw you!"

Tony grabbed her by the hair and demanded, "Are you involved in all of this?" When she didn't answer, he pushed her against the wall. He looked at her, and then without a word, he got in his car and left.

Charlene took a deep breath and closed the front door.

***

Tony went straight to his uncle's office at the Milione Casino. "I got a problem . . ." he began.

"I'll say," answered Marco. "You don't look so good. What's up?"

"You don't wanna know the details. I gotta find me a girl, a hooker. She screwed me over."

"You got screwed by a hooker?" Marco snickered. "Isn't that what you pay her for?"

"No, I mean—" sputtered Tony. "I need to find a hooker named Mysti. She fucking robbed me!"

Marco turned to his bodyguard. "Get the Kid on it. He's got contacts that know the whereabouts of all the working girls." Then he said to Tony, "You want us to handle her when the Kid finds her?"

"No!" exclaimed Tony. "I'll deal with her myself. Just tell me where she lives."

It didn't take long before the Kid's contacts came through. He was back with Mysti's address before Tony could finish his second drink.

Tony left the casino determined to hunt down Mysti.

***

It was late afternoon when Tony's silver Mercedes pulled up in front of the Rose Palace Hotel—Mysti's current place of residence, according to the Kid's source. Tony slammed through the front door and headed towards the stairs.

"Hey, who the hell are you?" The voice from the reception desk stopped him in his tracks. He turned around to see a fat guy yelling at him from behind the desk. His face was all red and soaked with sweat. "You can't just barge in like that."

Tony walked coldly towards the guy at the desk. "You know, I'm not in a very sociable mood today. And I need to recharge my battery on someone, and that someone just so happens to be you." He drew his hand back as if to give the guy a gentlemanly slap.

Tony barely broke stride. He threw a punch over the desk and knocked out the fat guy. Then he turned around, and he went up the stairs.

Mysti's room number was 201. They found the room and broke in the door. She was inside with a couple of her girlfriends, doing each other's hair. The girls started screaming, but Tony ignored them. "Where's Mysti?" Tony demanded.

He went straight for Mysti, who dove behind the bed when she saw him coming. "Bitch, there you are. You aren't leaving here alive."

He slapped her with his right hand and then backhanded her with even more force. "Where the fuck is my money, you stupid whore"

"Whore?" Mysti finished for him. She slowly stood up. "You gonna call me a whore? Ask me if I care."

Tony said nothing, but he raised his fist and moved towards her. "I don't give a fuck what you are. Where is my money?" He grabbed her by the upper arms and squeezed. She whimpered with the pain.

"I don't know. I don't know," she cried. "Stop hurting me. Please!"

Tony took a ten-dollar bill out of his pocket and waved it in front of her. "Will this help you talk, you stupid, cheap whore? Where's the money?" He hit her again.

Mysti turned her head away, crying. "I don't know! I don't know! All I know is that this Jack guy picked me up in a fucking Mercedes . . ."

"Mercedes, huh," said Tony. "We'll see about that." He realized he wasn't going to get anything more out of her. He hit her once more, knocking her onto the bed. Then he left.

He got in the car. He took out his cell phone and called someone. "It was that Jack guy," said Tony. "Jackpot, or whatever he called himself, drives a Mercedes Brabus. It was bought from us." He put the car in gear and peeled off from the curb. "So call our dealership and check it out. Get his address."

After a few minutes, his phone rang. "Boss, they don't have a Jack in the list of recent customers, but a Mercedes Brabus was recently purchased by a certain Peter Carter. Got his office address," said the caller.

Tony smiled for the first time that day. "Newton's third law," he said. "Every action has an equal and opposite reaction."

***

Pete was working late—at least that's what he'd told his wife—at his insurance office that evening. Though he was only there to set a few things in order, he was secretly planning to take his money and walk out of their nagging relationship. A customer had just been in, yelling about his payment or something. When Pete finally had enough, he sternly escorted the unhappy customer out the door, paying him farewell with a shouted, "I could cover your body with banknotes."

Good riddance, thought Pete, as he returned to his desk. He was just preparing to leave when Tony burst through the door. "Hello, Peter Carter. You thought you hit the jackpot, huh??!" said Tony, menacingly.

Tony put his mouth close to Pete's ear. "You're out of your league, office boy," he said in a low, menacing voice. "You shouldn't be pulling stunts that just prove somebody else's originality." He hit Pete's face with his elbow. "You robbed me, you fucker."

Blood started pouring out Pete's nose and down the front of his white shirt. Not wanting to stain his car with blood, Tony bundled Pete into the insurance executive's Mercedes and drove off. He stopped at a deserted rest area off the highway.

"Let me see you now, you pussy," snarled Tony as he yanked Pete out of the car. He pushed Pete into a metal guardrail. Pete's head crashed against the sign, and he fell down to his knees. Tony grabbed Pete by the ears and hauled him upright.

"Stand up!" ordered Tony. He slapped Pete with a fierce backhand. "Where's the money you stole from me? Do you hear me, asshole?"

"I don't have the money," Pete mumbled through his bleeding lips.

"You don't have my money? You screwing with me?"

Pete swallowed blood and tried to clear his throat. Pete finally found his voice. "Gene has it. He's got it."

"Gene?" a surprised Tony asked.

"The electronics genius. He's the one who hacked into your account."

"He's still alive? Is he some kind of a hidden genius now? Where is that motherfucker?" asked Tony.

"East side of town. I'm not sure; I don't have his full address." Pete fumbled for his cell phone, then held it out to Tony. "But I have his telephone number."

"Give me that phone." Tony grabbed it out of Pete's shaking hands. "Fuck, I got this prick's blood all over me."

Tony looked for and called Gene's number. The call connected. "Hello. You know who this is?" Tony said coldly.

"Sure," Gene answered.

"Where is my money? I'm counting to five. You spill it or I'll throw your pal off the overpass."

Pete heard this. "You gotta help me! Save me!" he called out, as if Gene could hear him through the phone.

Gene considered this. "How should I deliver the money to you?" he said when Tony had counted to four.

"Easy. Same way you stole it."

"Okay. The road where we dropped the papers."

"What are you talking about?"

"Pete knows, ask him."

Tony grabbed Pete's shirt. "What's he talking about? Where's the road where you dropped the papers?"

Pete looked bewildered. "What kind of papers?"

Tony sighed in exasperation. "What kind of papers?" he growled at Gene through the cell phone.

"His car ownership papers. We dumped them on the bridge," Gene said this with a satisfied smile on his face. His plans were coming together nicely.

Tony turned back to Pete. "Idiot, the bridge where you dumped the car's papers."

Pete brightened up. "Oh, I know! I know!" Finally, something he could answer.

"Then take me there," said Tony. He grabbed Pete and forced him back inside the Mercedes.

On the highway once more, Tony drove as he talked on the phone to Gene. "What now? How long is this road? It never ends. It's like we're driving to another country." He paused and nearly dropped the phone as he tried to wipe his hands. "Ugh, get your chicken shit blood off of me!"

Hearing this over the phone, Gene chuckled. He was in his apartment, watching his computer track the progress of the Mercedes Tony was driving, and he thoroughly enjoyed every minute of Tony's discomfort.

Tony heard Gene's soft laughter. "Hey, you laughing at me? You think this is some kind of a joke?" he snarled. "What now? You playing games with me?"

"Of course not." Gene was all seriousness now. "But I want to get something out of this, too."

"And what do you want?" asked Tony.

"First, dump my friend out on the street, and then we'll talk about it."

Tony reluctantly agreed. He hated taking orders from Gene, but it couldn't be helped. Besides, his prisoner by now was just a useless, bloody mess. He pulled the Mercedes over to the side of the road and kicked Pete out of the car. The Mercedes sped away, leaving Pete alone in the darkness.

In the car, Tony got back on the phone with Gene. "Okay, it's done. The garbage has been dumped. Where are you now?"

"I'm at the end of the bridge," Gene replied. "You have another mile to the bridge approach, and then come meet me at the end of the bridge. I'll be at the far end of the restaurant parking lot."

"You'd better be there," said Tony, menacingly.

"I will," answered Gene. "Trust me." He muted his phone but kept the line open, in case Tony needed further coaxing on the path to his destiny.

As the Mercedes cruised through the night, Tony finally felt like he was back in his groove. The car handled well; he was pushing its speed upward and passing other vehicles with ease. He was within yards of the bridge approach when he looked back and saw a police car behind him.

He pressed lightly on the accelerator, and the speedometer zoomed past 90 mph. A slow-moving truck loomed ahead of them, but Tony curved his car around it with the barest touch on the steering wheel. It was almost as if the Mercedes was driving itself.

In his apartment, Gene peered closely at the computer monitor. He was holding the phone with its MT8888 microchip; it was a very advanced version from his beloved game *Hugo*. He pressed the numbers 4 and 6 simultaneously on the phone's keypad. "Okay, get going, fast as you can," he whispered.

Gene's voice came over the cell phone that Tony had left open: "How's your navigator system working?"

The Mercedes was driving on its own. It veered to the left and glanced off the center-line guardrail, sending it back across the lanes to the right-hand shoulder and the edge of the bridge.

"What, aaaah . . . What the fuck is this? I can't control the car!" Tony said as he yanked at the steering wheel. Nothing happened. He hit it with the palm of his hand.

"Now!" said Gene, not caring whether Tony heard him or not. He pressed the "4" key.

The car's speed revved up, and it barreled across the width of the bridge at nearly a right angle, going head-on into the outer guardrail and flipping over it. The Mercedes turned end-over-end as it tumbled down forty feet through the air, landing upside down on the ground below, crushing Tony beneath its weight.

Chapter 12
Payoff

G ene was sitting in his apartment, listening to the TV announcer blather on:

> *New airbag designs for your car! This design allows quick escape, so there is no way you'll die inside your car—unlike the older airbags that trap you inside, where you cannot get out before the firemen arrive. The magic of these new airbags is that they have holes like straws for oxygen. Next, about their activation . . .*

The door opened, and Pete walked in. He was covered with bruises, and his clothing was torn and dirty. A few bloodstains spotted his shirt front.

"Do you know what happened?!" he exclaimed. "Didn't you see it on TV? Where's your fucking remote?"

"What?" said Gene. "Here's the remote on the table."

"Which one? There's so many of them."

"The silver one."

Pete picked up the remote and clicked through the channels, looking for the latest in local news.

> *The elusive Tony Donatelli, an alleged mob king, got killed today in a vehicular accident. He was believed to be connected to the Mafia and was a suspect in a lottery scam years ago.*

Gene took the remote from Pete and turned off the TV. "So, how did he crash?" he asked, pretending not to have a hand in Tony's fate.

"Lost control of his car while speeding across the bridge," answered Pete. "Flipped over the guardrail and landed upside down on the ground forty feet below. Crushed by the car. Nothing left of him."

Gene shook his head and sighed. Then he looked at Pete. "Shame about that 850."

"That wasn't a BMW; it was my Mercedes!"

"Oh, sorry, how many Mercedes are you going to lose?" Gene smiled, handing Pete a bag stuffed with bills. "That should help you deal with your client who has to be paid. And there's a little extra . . ."

"To start a new life?" Pete asked hopefully.

"To start a new life," Gene nodded. "Come back here for more."

Pete took the bag, gave Gene a mock salute, and walked out the door.

Alone now, Gene walked aimlessly around the apartment. He opened a cash bag and looked at the stacks of cash stored within. He picked up a handful of bills and smelled them. "Not a bad consolation prize," he said.

Suddenly, he noticed a loud buzzing from a fly trapped inside the window. He grabbed a flyswatter and held it menacingly over the insect. The insect landed on the windowsill and stopped buzzing. Then Gene tossed the flyswatter aside and opened the window to let the fly out.

"There's been enough death for one day," he said as he closed the window and went back to his computer.

Chapter 13
The Dock, Revisited

It was late in the afternoon one summer when the ferry boat from the big cruise ship pulled up at the dock in the little Sicilian port town. Charlene got off with the rest of the passengers, but she didn't stay with the crowd of tourists looking for places to dine and shop. She liked the cruise all right—especially the food, the casino, and the nightlife—but she'd had enough of rubbing elbows with her fellow passengers.

She needed to stretch her legs, so she decided to walk down to the far end of the dock where it was less crowded. Only a few locals were about, some fishing and others just strolling along like Charlene. The sun had begun its glorious descent, slowly erasing the blue sky and painting it a cool orange, purple, and red.

Fashionably dressed and carrying an elegant leather handbag over her shoulder, Charlene stared out to the sea. She pulled something out of her handbag—it was the silver wallet that the young Tony retrieved for her when it fell into the waters by the dock. She found it in one of the boxes in Tony's house while she was helping his family sort out his things. She wished she had known about the wallet earlier in their relationship.

Tears started rolling down her eyes. Charlene looked down at the silver wallet in her hand. *"Ciao,"* she whispered. She pulled her arm back, and, with all her might, threw the wallet far out into the water. *"Ciao,"* she said again, *"Ciao, Siciliano."*

The End